MEAT TOOTH

a love letter

MEAT TOOTH

a love letter

Jeff Senatra

EMPTY HANDS ETC. PRESS

I've no story to tell because there are no stories, no ends, only snapshot phantasms like clouds—vaporous driftings billowing by on their way to the great dissolve.

HUNT

Now

              scattered on garden earth

   where it's all a search

      one grand and terrible

            continuous

       hunt

here

    in this city

   this

night

it's stopped

raining.

Everywhere is wet wet. Puddles reflect streetlights like sad electric moons, and trees drip in the dark. Listen... hear the thin sick sound of splatter against the sidewalk like slow century ticks of time...

Moving through this night is like probing to find the cunt of an octopus. Though the air is light and cool the clouded swarthiness of the sky lays like a big fat Arab cadaver on a slab of marble. It's heavy, wants to roll over and fall on my head, crush me suffocate me in the dark cavernous rolls of its flesh. I walk along 18th Street with my head down like the prow of a ship plowing sludge. In the street at night alone I am free, I am immune. With the collar of my jacket up over my jaw, head bowed eyes rolled upward I am a sleek beast snarling at the drawn boundary circle of the world and those comfortable within its fat perimeter; a sleek beast turning away from all landscapes to roam alone. A smile stretches my cheeks at this thought and I lift my head into the blackness. Black sorrow, triumphant night, liberator...Stare into the darkness womb surrounding me and think about the world as man has made it and how it was actually meant for man. We have been flung too far from the initiates of the sun. Nature refuses to claim us as its own. We've become small and putrid. We look at nature as if it were a sideshow freak, as if we are separate from it. We point at it and laugh. And in turn nature seals us from the portal of its womb. Mother abandons child with a sad snarl tangled in her throat. We have been abandoned, and we are lost.

Black sorrow, triumphant night, liberator…Night drops like a friendly black baby shark upon the city and caresses with its swim, encloses us in its tough circle like an ever widening pupil, hiding us, waking the buildings into their yellow-eyed guardian selves. Night defies the rank pearly spread of dawn's wings to show themselves but always the wings come fearless and confident and unshaken, unfolding sleepily rising like a hot blue star over the bent-headed silhouetted land. Dawn comes always and kicks night out of the garden with a snicker, rebirth, and begins the whole roll of the game all over again. Each day is a new confusion, new suicide.

Black sorrow, triumphant night, liberator…What is it falling in our chalice? Golden paratroopers descend with skull eyes. Green old men monster faces stare out from the child's window without so much as a whisper as to which direction befalls the moan, the man, the moon. The rags of Time wrap round our limbs to drag us off. The feathered chariot carrying our dreams is broken with weight falling to the kiss of the cannibal, the enemy among us who is never ever suspected of treason and murder, and that enemy is ourselves.

Black sorrow, triumphant…What dear force there is

in the lightest of touch. What dark resources springing in the mind like a sizzling river of voices. What honor we hold in ourselves, what blind knowledge, a hundred million eyes all watering with laughter at once, and what blind pain, and longing…But longing for what? What is it we need? Answers, yes, the kind we can touch. Like doves we'd stroke their backs and watch them fly toward the gold of the sun. And freedom certainly…to live forever in the manner each of us desires for ourselves without fear or condemnation or ennui or capitulation to the impending trap.

Black sorrow…The horror is not only horror but whorefaced niggership. We, all of us are niggers— slaves to Time and the restless upheaval of the yawning jaws signaling the end, the spread-eagled grave moistening up more and more each day for our entry; slaves to societal politics, tradition, family, friendship, success, failure, love, illusion. I've discovered my problem. I don't want to be a big man and take on this world. This world is backward and insane it's terrifying. I feel like I have to be someone else to live in it. I don't want that. I want the long-legged lotus dream, the opium dream of childhood. I want to live like a golden child under secure blankets of warm earth rhythms, immune. There's a huge cavity of hell raging within me, a boiling vat of fear just under the surface. Sometimes I can control it and things seem fine and manageable, but then suddenly without warning I explode with anxiety and howl and rip at the walls as tears collect in my eyelids like black tadpoles straight from the Lower Empire. The only alleviation for this hell is the street. In the street, at night, alone, I am free. I am immune.

Heading down 18th toward Guerrero, usual route. Could do it in my sleep; nearly have on occasion. Just past Dolores Street at the Bi-Rite market cross to the left side of 18th then down to Guerrero where I hang a left and BANG, like the bright full moon stepping out naked from a thick house of clouds to reveal its neon breasty beam, just like that the sparkling neon sign hits me from a block away. As I approach, the big pink and gold neon cocktail glass reflects shimmeringly like liquid, like a blurry promise or dreamy mirage of comfort and forthcoming drink pleasure, transfiguration, in the first story windows of the apartment building across Guerrero. I notice it every time I come walking up—moves along the windows like a shaky cartoon. That's where Joe lives, the bartender. They're his windows that reflect the sign like a red cross burned into the forehead. He must roll out of bed some days and gag in his morning (which for him is late afternoon) shot of scotch seeing that sign day in day out, probably even in his sleep. 500 Club. I look into the windows of the bar as I pass. Nah…too early. I hang a left back up 17th then hook over to the right up Dolores. The sky is turning deep blue now and a few stars are letting tiny sighs go through breaks in the gray clouds above the feathered tops of the fat palm trees fanning over the median. At the median's separation I veer across the street toward the old Mission Dolores chapel gaping like a huge bleached skull in a toothless silent howl. On the broad doorstep of the church next to the chapel homeless in sleeping bags huddle in the shadows. Another left at 16th and one block more I see the J train approaching as it crawls up Church Street, and I board.

*

My slightly blurred reflection looks on coolly beside me in the night train window. I'm slumped, boot and jeaned leg resting 4-shaped over a knee. My ghost in the window looks sinister, bored and sad. My eyes are sunken vacuum halls of horror. I don't care…Two Hispanic women board at Market, pass me and fill my nose with sick strangling perfume. STRONG. Makes me gag. The art of the scent is a delicate matter, requires some intuitive sensitivity and horse sense. All these women and men too with their colognes dousing themselves so that they burn the eyes of every person they pass as if exuding radiation waves will they never understand that it's the freshness up-close subtlety that's enticing, not the sledgehammer rain? Obviousness is only attractive to the obvious. The good fresh scent preciously of you, you had a light touch, you understood. Can still smell it now…No I can't that was a lie. But I remember laying my face against your neck and breathing under your hair.

This train is a worm, big fat gliding roaring burrowing earthmouthed two-headed earthworm slugging its way across pavement across city across the night, leaving a slime trail of steel rails shining under streetlights. Worm digs thickly now as if through a fallen monster's black heart and emerges from the tunnel underground into the sleepy light of Van Ness station. A beautiful girl sits all alone on a bench waiting for her train. I stare hard at her through the glass and shoot thoughts at her mind but she won't lift her turn her nose to my window, won't return my love in my window, why do they never look into my window!

*

Hop off at the next stop, Civic Center, decide to zigzag through the Tenderloin. When I climb to the top of the steps out of the underground onto Market Street a guy standing there at the entrance lets little purple moths with machineguns go from the side of his mouth as I pass: Outfits outfits, clean outfits. Red-rimmed crocodile eyes skimming through blackwater skin. I ain't no fuckin junky, I say. No reply, doesn't care one way or another. Just out here feeding the streets so the streets will feed him. Honest work for honest death. Smell of urine-splattered storefronts. There's slick film in spots coating the sidewalk. I slip now and then. God*dammit!* Take the next left off Market and head into the black meat of it.

Deeper into the interior, the smooth black ride lost— I decide to head for Geary some blocks away and walk that down. Dark streets, dark climb, black guys with 40s clinging to sides of buildings and corner bodega entrances. Hey man, one guy says, you need queens?

Codeine? Shake my head. Each shadow conceals a gun and clubbing, a pimp, a punk, whore ghost and angel. If I *make it* to Geary, that is.

Pass a small clump of Filipinos. Girl climbs onto the back of a guy for a ride. They're pushing and pulling one another, rapping. They're bored, waiting for something to come along and present itself in the night. I offer myself like a Eucharist. As I pass I can feel their surreptitious eyes and energy fiercely swirl about me. I'm gonna go make some *money* I hear one say, and begins to follow. I don't turn around. Let him pursue me. Hunk of fish bait dragging through the ocean and a barracuda has just picked up the scent. His energy is a blowtorch at my back. Wallet chain jingles against his baggy thigh. Now and then the soles of his shoes scrape the sidewalk. Well you're finally gonna get it. You've been pushing it long enough now you're finally gonna get it. Alright. So be it. My money the few bucks I've got is his money. It's communal. Let him come and get it. Come on kill me for it fucker. My heart's a marching drum corps gone berserk. Though I'm about to get a knife in the ribs I like it, I like knowing that I am alive. I like my vital signs kicking me in the ass and wiping the sleep and glue out of my eyes. Let things happen to you is my approach. Death isn't even a consideration really. Fear of death would block all necessary experience. You've got to give yourself up completely to that huge hand of life and just let it guide you along like a stick in a river. And if it refuses to take you over if it refuses to lead...well, that's when you insist upon it. Get up there in its fat corroding slothy face and scream MARCH! Move on! Either up or down but never deadly still never like an ugly pond laced with buggy scum. No. Demand your life simply by letting life happen. This is what you came here for now let's see what's gonna occur, let's see how you're gonna handle it. Walk on. Trolling bait. Barracuda closing in. Grip the Bic lighter in my jacket pocket and make a fist in there. Poor substitute for a roll of coins but should do. Should get points for ingenuity at least. Points from who? I always feel like there's someone watching me, some invisible entity looming over my shoulder from behind the curtain of another dimension, observing, judging in a nonjudgmental way if that makes any sense, like a priestly scientist. He, It, doesn't do anything, it's just there, as if it were a secret but very natural part of my own being and I'm taking notes on myself to understand. Under the nearest streetlight suddenly I whirl, fist out like a feeble flesh hammer. Face it head on that's it. Accelerate the life process by jerking death off. Stare into the black long enough and the colors will come. But when I spin there's no one there. Immune. I am immune. Musta smelled humanity's thumbprint poverty on me like a dogshit stench and gave it up, like a rodent smells human fondling on her young and eats it.

The drum corps of my heart on the other hand doesn't quit. It keeps marching on and pounding away till finally after a couple blocks it takes a left turn while I take a right and lose it.

I keep going that way, a left here, right there, down this block, hmmm here's a nice dark one, down a little further, wading through that dimness forest like a slit-eyed snake pit, buildings seething dense tree patches from which panthers jump for the jugular. Senses large I go eyeing shadows and faces and hands furtively till I get to Geary where there's a bit more activity and light.

*

Geary now. Hey, Red Man! What's *he* doing here? Flits past me like a whacked-out red and black specter. Same get-up he's usually in, face and hands painted blaring red as a screaming fire truck, heavy black eyeliner, dyed coal-black hair and pencil mustache, sunken Artaud cheeks, wearing a red silk bathrobe and knocking ash with a single tap of his index finger from a cigarette stuck in a long black holder. Looks like Salvador Dali imitating an aristocratic lobster. Never says a word. Only see him in the Mission, what's he doing in the Tenderloin? I turn to look back at him but he's disappeared into the murk.

Prostitutes on every other corner, in doorway alcoves or walking in slow shortskirted tandem pairs. Guy in tie and crisp white shirt in a white SUV is pulled along the curb. In a white mini a blonde leans in through the open passenger door window. How bout a blowjob then? she says. Huh?...40...Yeah a blowjob's 40...

I get hard immediately when I hear her say it but the SUV creeps off, not going for it. Pausing, I rub my crotch standing on the sidewalk.

Whore in white mini is joined by a brunette wearing the same skirt only black. Oooo my feet hurt, Blondie whines as Blackie comes walking up, these darn corns…Well when you get home tonight, Blackie says, soak'em in hot water with Epsom salts…Just then an old red raspy guy rolls up in a brown Cadillac, face like a big mashed up cranberry squeezed juiceless behind the wheel. Hey! he gargles. Where's your high heels at tanight! Blondie has kicked off her shoes and is standing in nylons on the cold concrete. There's a band-aid stuck high up on her right calf beneath her stocking. Ah fuck off tanight Frank! she yells. Just fuck off! AH HA HA HUH he laughs. Last thing I need tonight is you squirt'n between my toes! AHHUHARRR Frank laughs again, and slowly rolls on…

With an erection then pointing my way I continue down Geary. From the opposite side of the street I'm in the sights of another blonde, caught me glancing over. Keen eye the whore possesses like a hawk, or poet. Where'ya goin? she calls. Twist my neck smile jut my jaw out ahead in a nod and say not quite loud enough for her to hear over the chasm of the street, I'm just walkin. I'm playing with her now. The gesture I just made was a signal she understands, one she's used to. Covert flag of procedure. She thinks she's found experience a real class A or at least class *B* date. Doesn't realize it's the stockings not the scissoring legs of the woman in the stockings that fascinate me, heavy black swirling lace like iron lattice work—viny trellis leaned against the house of her leading back to the garden window. Women ache to be like the earth, and men seek passage back to the womb. Well slow down Honey! she calls again. She crosses the street behind me. Gaping wound in heels, city earth personified, bastardized earth, controlled environment, a gouge in the pavement where a few weak blades of grass sprout, yields everything to you for the proper exchange if you don't mind the pillaging of your emotions and mind. Nonetheless my erection throbs and I can't help rubbing it in sneaky little rubs. Ya gonna slow down or *what!* Natural stride neither fast nor slow, not my fault she's in spike heels. I'll do her with a pool cue but that's about all and then only for free. Laugh thinking of Matisse making drawings from five feet away with a piece of charcoal tied to a long stick. Does she see me laughing? Track star. Chases me a full two blocks (Better slow down, Hon!) before splitting off.

*

On the inside glass of the door to a diner a sweaty woman in a white apron tapes a sign that says *Cheryl's baby was a girl! Born 4/18.*

Welcome to the furnace little one.

In the window a huge turkey brown and shiny roasts like a bound up little child. Cherry pie slice in a cooler to the right sits with thick cream on top, red filling infiltrating the cream like splattered blood. My lips melt into shallow pools; I go in and order tea and pie. Would like more, but wanna save the rest of my cash for beer. Black guy in drag comes in sashaying like a swing between two men. They arrive together arms linked and stand at the entrance waiting to be seated. The old Greek behind the counter waves them away. They look at each other easily, laugh, then saunter out the way they came in.

*

On Grant Street Chinatown's a dusky oyster that's clamped itself shut on the slimy luster of its pearl. Most of the shops and markets are closed and the tourists have wandered off. An old man drunk and shaky leans a hand against a lamppost outside the Buddha Bar and screams to the night I KNOW WHAT'S GOING ON!...I *KNOW* WHAT THE *FUCK'S* GOIN ON!...I *KNOW*...I KNOW *WHAT'S...GOING...ON!...I* know ...what's...—His voice trails off crinkling up like old used tin foil and flakes away into garbage pit nothingness. Stands there leaning heavily staring down at the wet street, silent. No more words, no more screams, lets night take the conversation now. He listens.

*

Strip Clubs on Broadway are twinkling their cool bosom neons white and red through verdure leaves of the plants sprouting like long pointy donkey ears on the window ledge near my table in the bar across Columbus where I sit. The neon is smearing wet Broadway with strange shiny carpets. Faces flash by outside as I lift pint after pint, spend the rest of my money. The faces pause now and then and peer wide-eyed lonesome numb into the window in front of me as if to ask is this it? Is this the place where my soul and steps can sleep and lift the bane and lame world cantor circling my weary brow? No, my eyes tell them, it is not.

Lovers hand in hand on the street strolling on their smile way to heaven lovebeds where life culminates in the joy of brief and this is the world the whole world and they know. In the quiet still warmness of love between a couple, any couple, lies the brilliance of God, any god. My god where are you and what are you doing now this very moment in this same country on this same continent on this same planet so far away! My hand is empty!

Now and then we must allow ourselves the luxury of grieving for ourselves. I am grieving.

Girls pace in the bright entryways of the strip clubs showing lots of thigh and glittery faces, eyes painted falsely hungry, calling to guys that pass on the sidewalk, spiders singing to flies, like at a carnival the men that stand at their booths chanting and soliciting you to come take a crack at their stupid games, trying to sucker you in. Even as a kid I wouldn't fall for that shit, saw right through it. Guess I've always been a grumbling old man...

*

Back in the underground at 4th and Market, walking

through the long corridor. The walls are puffed in hard honeycomb tile-bubbles like white blind enamel insect eyes staring at me. Eerie feeling of walking through a catacomb of gigantic prehistoric locust skins that at any moment could reawaken to animated life. Grimy bearded men stretch along the floor against the walls passing a pint of vodka. One among them stands in the corridor on wobbly legs digging and tugging inside the seat of his jeans. With every tug he throws himself headfirst toward the floor but manages to catch himself with his other hand. A last mighty pull deposits him flat out face down where, with a weary sigh of triumph, he extracts a strip like beef jerky from his pants—lays it on the ground before him.

I hop the turnstile, no attendant, and head back across town. My only chance for more drinks tonight is the 500 Club.

*

That sign again like a big neon elixir homage raised in a toast to the gods; that sign a red harlot seduction, beacon, electric life raft…Gold light bubbles blink on and off inside the cocktail glass like fireflies mad on meth trapped in a jar.

Busier now. Thick smoke tumbles through the open door like a drunken ghostship crew of pirates bearing gray velour sacks of looted music and laughter. Spaceman at the end of the bar circling a lit match around his head to ward off evil, talking about whorehouses on Mars. And I'm the only one who knows where they are, right? And the government knows this, right? And keeps sending me letters of request, see? Asking will I please work with NASA, confidentially of course, cuz the president wants to try some of this Martian pussy. Like he should, right? Cuz man I tell ya, ain't nothing like these cathouses on Mars. Nothing like it, right?… He's trapped the couple next to him in conversation. The guy gives him one blind ear and nods continually while keeping a watchful eye on his girl who smiles broadly as I pass. I look at her and smile back. Hmmm…Finding an empty spot at the middle of the bar I stand there. Out of the corner of my eye I see her turn toward me.

YOU! OUT! YOU *ASSHOLE!*

Behind the bar Joe's eyes are blue druid fire, his nose a winter horse's flared nostrils pouring out steam. Guy passing behind me stops in his tracks. Room goes still, except for the idiot jukebox which never does know when to shut up.

THE NEXT TIME YOU GO INTO THE LADIES ROOM, Joe shouts, YOU BETTER HAVE A *PUSSY!*

Men's room was full, the guy offers as meek defense.

OUT! YOU FFFFUCKING ASSHOLE! GET OUT! Joe fixes the intense flame of his gaze until its heat forces the guy to slink off. Fffucking prick, Joe mutters, wiping the bar. AND DON'T COME BACK TIL TAMARRA NIGHT! Blu…

Just as dainty as you please Joe turns to me from this

exchange, smile breaking on his lips like the soft crack of a baby's doughy behind.

Gin and tonic Blu? he asks.

I'm tapped Joe.

Turns his smile upside down, nods. Sawright, he says. Makes the drink. There ya go Starry Eyes.

All gin, dash of tonic. Ahhh home. I shift an eye to the end of the bar toward Spaceman and the couple. Shit. The couple's collecting their things to leave. I watch the beauty of the girl until she disappears through the door shaking her long brown hair behind her. And oh that smile…

Likes to call me that for some reason—rrrrrrrrrrrr—Starry Eyes—rrrrrrrrrrrrrrrrrrr—don't know why—rrrrr-RRRRRRR—I must look pretty out of RRRRRRR-RRRRRRAAARRRRRRRK—RARK—*What the fuck!*

I look over and Bug's eyes like crazy ferris wheels are spinning up at me from the next stool, hadn't seen him in all the commotion. He's laughing. His long wispy gray beard swabs around his face like soiled gauze in tatters. I did that once yehs ago in a bah in Nahlins man, he laughs. No one knew me, just stahted bahkin at the bah AH HA HA…Tru me ahta there brotta AH HA…Howya doin there Blu?

Pretty good. I'm immune.

Wah?

Nothin.

Speakin'a Nahlins, Blu I ever tell ya bout Weepin Willy Wilson? Buddy a mine. This hahse race they just had on the tube heah reminded me ov'im. He an I was stationed down in Nahlins nineteen sixty two I think it was or some goddamn thing, stayed in the same roomin house down theah, both waitin for a ship. Hell we shipped all ovah the goddamn place tagethah. Singapooah, motherfuckin Is-tan-bul. Anyway, Weepin Willy played the hahses, see? Now when I say he played the hahses I mean I saw'im win a hunnerd an fifty thousand dollahs one day. I mean that guy knew what he was doin. Won big all the fuckin time—

Why'd they call him *Weeping* Willy then? I ask.

Cuz when he lost, maaaan…he lost *big*. He was a little nuts, see? Well ya hafta be ta bet like that guy did. He'd lose all his money, I mean flat busted broke, his whole month's pay, then he'd come round ta us guys fa cash. I toll'im one time Willy I ain't *got it*. Then he stahted goin through my room want'na pahn shit. I had ta slug'im ta get'im outta my room. An he stahted bahlin right theah in the hallway outside my dooah. Man I tell ya I felt like shit. But what could I do? I didn't have nutt'n.

But when'ee won…and most the time he did win, the fuckah most all the time had a lump a cash ahn'im …One time he says ta me Bugs c'mahn less go ta dinnah, less get a steak. A STEAK I says, Willy I ain't got no money fa that shit. Ahn me he says. Fuckin guy. Big shot, see? But he was awright like that man. If he had the bucks his buddies were with'im all the way. He didn't give two shits about it. Money wasn't nutt'n ta him. So he takes me out ta this hotel, the Richmond I think it was called, riziest joint in town at one time, and that goddamn guy we're HUH…we're sittin there in the restrant, an Willy's orderin Dom Periom or some shit, all the expensive stuff, and we're fucked up, see? And here comes this waitress and puts these drinks ahn our table and I go what's this? Willy we order these? Naw he says, and the waitress goes these are from mista Frank Sinatra, he's about ta puhfahm an he baht the house a round a drinks. Well that goddamn Willy goes TAKE'M BACK! He's yellin TAKE'M BACK! I don't know nutt'n from no Frank Sinatra! he goes. And here, he says, trows down a coupla hunnerds ahner tray, give the house a round on *me*, Willy Wilson. HA HA that sonofabitch I tell ya wasn't gonna be out done by *no*body…Wannanotha drink therah Blu? Joe! Two mooah heah!

Joe brings a Bud for Bugs and another gin and tonic for me. That fuckin Spaceman, Joe says, that fucker's down there scarin all deese young girls. I've had tree complaints already. I gotta get'im outta here man he's gonna drive me nuts. He's down there tellin every girl that sits down beside'im that he's God and do they wanna work on Mars or some goddamn ting I don't know.

I look up the bar. Spaceman's sitting there like a pale placid mountain serenely waiting for the clouds to get out of his hair, an empty stool on either side of him, cradling his beer in a ham hock fist like it was one of those miniature bottles of booze you get on airplanes. Big *big* guy. Then I see the girl from before is back sitting in the same place she was earlier near Spaceman and sipping at a shot. Don't see the guy around though. She turns my way and smiles. Seems pretty quiet now, I say staring back at her.

Yeah well the motherfucker one more complaint and the whole lot of him goes, Joe says, walking out from behind the bar and around the corner to the backroom. Comes back a few minutes later sniffing and rubbing his nose.

Joe who's that girl down there?

Which?

By Spaceman, the one sippin that shot a...what's that...vodka?

Oh yah, he says. That's the Russian.

The *who?*

The Russian's nipples poke at the inside of her black tshirt like Moe at Curly's eyes. What the hell, I'm staring. On her shirt printed in white outline is a reproduction of a Picasso drawing, centaur carrying off a naked woman—I let that be my guide.

As if her breasts are large comely magnets and my eyes shiny though slightly smudged steel balls I find myself drawn up bar staring them in the eye. I come up stand beside her bend my face down in her chest and roll my eyes around. When I raise my gaze she's smiling down at me. Sorry, I say straightening myself upright, I was just admiring your uh shirt. Picasso.

That's alright, she says thrusting her chest forward, and the drawing expands. Take a look. Do you like Picasso?

Mmmmhmm

Well what else do you like?

Well I don't know. What's your name?

You can call me Fab.

Why would I do that?

That's my name, Fabrianasha. I'm from Moscow. I came to San Francisco on tour with my ballet troop but I quit to stay here. I lahhve America.

You mean you defected?

They no longer call it that.

Oh yeah right. I forgot.

They call me Fab because it's too hard to remember my real name. Too long, too many…um, syb…syballuls?

Syllables.

Yes syllables. Oh you're so nice. And pretty too. My English is not so good yet.

I think you're doing great.

I say Fab to make it easy. Sounds more American, yes?

No. I won't call you that.

What?

You know what that is? A fucking detergent. An American soap product that people wash their clothes with. You want to be called after a detergent?

She looks at me with no expression whatsoever,

nothing but blank. I mean her eyes don't even sparkle or face twitch or anything. Just nothing, there's nothing there. Like I could knock on her forehead and it'd make the same sound as if I'd rapped on the bar. It's as if for her time has suddenly ceased and she is trapped frozen like a photograph, all energies suddenly sucked from her command. But then, it's weird, just as suddenly she smiles and the gift of animation flushes through her being again and the corners of her teeth shine with little red green blue and white stripes reflected from the big-bulbed Christmas lights strung above around the entire rectangle of the ceiling—life restored. Where'd you go, I say, you scared me for a second.

Oh you're so niiice, she says placing her hand lightly against my chest, leaving it there. What's your name?

Blu.

Bluuu, she says. Her fingers are like feathers. Her eyes dance at me and her smile widens. Then her eyes dance harder, more wild and out of control. They start doing sweaty jungle gyrations. They clasp onto mine and refuse to let go and pull me into the fire of their circle. Then she cocks her head and leans over and kisses me. Slowly from my chest her hand begins to glide to my belly, then over my belly to my belt, and then under my belt right down inside my jeans. I can feel her hand fishing around in there. When it gets hold of what it's seeking it adjusts the object upward. She strokes slowly at first, still smiling into my eyes, then quickly picks up the pace. Faster and faster.

Mmmmmmmmmmmmmmmmmmmmmmmmm

I lean close to both her and the bar to block the view from the booths behind us and put one boot on the foot rail so that my thigh hides what's going on from the other customers seated at the bar. My eyes close. I hunch over and my head hangs down loose. I begin to feel the escape. This girl's hand is taking me somewhere. I feel myself ooze out of my skin like vapor and rise toward the ceiling. Like an invisible kite I rise soaring from the cluttered basement of the physical plane to the attic ascent of some astral mansion filled with nothing but huge echoing space. For a moment, for one brief shining moment I leave the smoke and noise and faces of that bar and achieve pure silent essence flow. With each pump of the Russian's hand I go higher and higher, further into the stratosphere, further away from this world and my life in it into the clean womb of nonbeing. I hear nothing. The sharp sounds of the bar are gone replaced by distorted silence, like being submerged in water. I'm gone and free and floating, real. The same type of real I experience when sleep has immersed me deep in dream and I feel like I've finally reached the center point, I've finally reached the place where I open and there is no *I* anymore only truth, only unrational unsubstantiated unattached nothingness of truth that ironically reattaches you to everything that is wholly life. I don't want to come back. I never want to come back.

Suddenly though I feel a familiar pull from deep

inside my body, which is somewhere way down there but somehow we are still attached—a pull tugging me backwards. And with the recognition of this sensation all at once I am descending, sucked back down to earth. Falling, falling. Ah Icarus my brother I'm right behind you! The smoky plumes of your burning wings are stinging my eyes. I'll piss on them and put the fire out.

The smoke and noise begin to seep back into my senses. I become more aware now of a foreign hand jammed into my pants. Discomfort replaces bliss. It's no use, I'm back. The drinks rise in my bladder swelling to flood. I lean my head to hers and say, I...uh... have to go to the bathroom.

Parting curtain her smile draws wide again and slowly like a snake leaving its hole her hand slithers away.

I go take my piss, the bubbles on the water when I pee look like violent frog eggs, drop some quarters in the condom machine, nothing comes in return, curse it and give it a good smack, fucking thing, go back out to the Russian edge up to her real close at the bar kiss some more play discretely with her breasts a little and finish my drink in between. Listen I only live a few blocks from here, I say, why don't we go to my place? Well she says looking at her watch I want to fuck you but I'm supposed to meet some friends. We kiss some more and I rub her crotch a little and she says OK. On the way out I tell her go ahead I'll be right with her and whisper to Tony, another bartender at the 500 Club, not working tonight though just in drinking, young pretty boy street punk, not very tall but solid and powerful looking, thick sausage fingers, like a wallop from him would cave your ribcage in as if there were iron-ore and lightning bolts in his knuckles, wears a 50s style felt hat most the time, generally he's a cocky little prick but I like him, there's strength and confidence in his presence, I whisper to him and he shouts WHADDAYA NEED? A RUBBER? I grit my teeth at him through a smile and fortunately the Russian has already stepped out onto the street and while Tony laughs he pulls out his wallet and hands over a couple of Sheiks and I catch up with the Russian and Tony's still laughing as I go through the door the fucking turd.

On the walk over I put my arm around her and try to hold her hand and she goes so ro*man*tic and smiles that goddamn smile at me, but this time a bit nervously, like I'm doing something wrong and making her uneasy, like she's beginning to think I'm taking this thing a bit too seriously. So I place my hand on her waist again spanning the small of her back and let it slide lower and strangely now she seems more relaxed.

I look up at the sky and it is still a blue and gray jigsaw puzzle.

At the apartment we head straight to my bedroom in the dark. We begin on the floor. Picasso comes off immediately bless his wild-eyed skin. Then off comes my shirt. Then the genie pants she is wearing unsnap and I dip into the honey pot and paddle my finger around and

I'm licking her nipple and she goes do you know Death In Venice?

Mmm? I go.

Thomas Mann, she says.

Whaw?

Do you like Thomas Mann?

Spit the nipple out and lift my head and look at her. Yeah I like Hermann Hesse too but why do you bring it up now? Not giving her a chance to answer I scoop her tiny body up in my arms and plop her on the bed and pull the rest of our clothes off. There's only room for one literary freak at a time and at the moment I'm occupied.

I unroll one of the Sheiks.

What's that? You don't need that, I don't *have* anything.

Neither do I. Like to keep it that way.

Plunge in.

But she won't give it up so easily, the literary talk.

I *lahhve* Thomas Mann *UH!*...I jab her with it... Mmmmmyou know, she says slowly, languishingly, sending each word out like a puff of cloud, he is my faaaavrit...mmmmmmmmmmmmmmuHA! Gave her a good one that time. And another and another.

Then she laughs.

What? I say.

No response. I keep right on.

She laughs again.

Why do you laugh?

What…she says…I wait for more but that's the only word that floats from her mouth. We bounce on.

You're laughing, I say. Why do you laugh?

My face is buried in her hair. It has trapped within it cigarette smoke and something that smells like rude incense. Her head is firmly wrapped in the coils of my arms. What's the matter? she says. I'm having a good time.

Yeah? You mean when you laugh you're coming?

Uh-huh…

Oh…Not the usual response ya know…

Pumping pumping fast in the dark trying to regain momentum trying to split the Russian apart, to obliterate the rose and lay the wet strewn petals right in the dewy hand of the great Mother ecstatic, fighting the wilting irony of the laughter swirling around my head in the darkness like a corona of mosquitoes, fighting to feel through the rubber sheath strangling my cock, behind my eyes your face looms like the transparent umbrella of a jellyfish engulfing its dinner. The delicious words you'd purr in my ear when we made love blaze through my brain like a lit-up marquee—deeeperr …deeeperr…fuck me deeeperrrr…—and my bone machine pushed to probe further into your body tunnel, into your viscera, toward the light, the source…The prolonged throaty gasp you'd emit with each orgasm, that lilting half-smile you'd use afterwards while staring into my eyes to tell me you loved me, the look, because words simply could not contain it all, all the emotion you wished to convey, couldn't express what you wanted to give to me like a half-melted candy heart, had to use your eyes to tell me...Then, like a shy little girl handing a valentine to a boy you have a crush on, you'd raise your shoulders to your chin like snuggling with yourself because you felt so warm inside you didn't know what else to do, and I'd hold you and stroke your hair and kiss your neck, cheek...The longing for you, for those eyes, ripe ember glow, desert vigil, green sirocco, mild incantation, it's you I crave, to eat, the fruit bite bright nibble of your throat, ear, the rich birdie valley of your belly, the verdant earth roll of your hips to lavender to ease rollicking forward, the teeth gleam bit of your breasts rising in a chant of pillows majesty mountain sunbeam marshmallow peaks and I glide...I glide...over your dew meadow...long... Pushing pushing I've nothing left, no more laughter from the Russian only weak pushing, feeble pushing... rubbery...roll off...

We lie beside each other breathing in the dark. A green sulfurous flash from the J train rumbling down the hill of Dolores Park across the street from my apartment and roaring on up Church Street illuminates the room like gangrene lighting up the blood. The building quivers. Rumbling of the train reverberates through my chest. The Russian's hand nests itself like a sparrow on my stomach as her face nestles to my shoulder. Mmm-mmmmmmmm she goes, then—Why did it get so soft toward the end?

I hate these fucking things, I sigh, tugging off the dead slimy snake skin and tossing it to the floor.

It's started raining again. The wind blows a fine spray against the windows.

Oh I'm so lazy toniiight, she says, and I like the way she said it—*toniiight*, stretching out the vowel sound. Something about it seems so childlike, like sleepy innocence rubbing its eyes. There's so much I wanted to do, she says, but—stretches her arms over her head, smiles, eyes twinkling in the darkness like the silver beads of rain on the window—I just feel so laaazy.

What did you do when you left the bar earlier? With that guy you were with?

What? Why?

I just want to know.

You're craazyy.

Tell me.

I think…he is…voy…voyeur?

Voyeur? Whaddaya mean?

Smiles secretively, shrugs.

Tell me. What did you do?

Shrugs again.

You mean, you touched yourself and he watched?

Nods like a gleeful chipmunk, eyes two black diamonds gleaming. Yes he took me to his car parked just down the street. I got in the back and he was in the front, and he watched me. He put his chin on the back of his seat and he watched from there. I didn't mind. Then I got out and he drove away and I went back inside the 500.

On her again in a flash. Unroll the other Sheik but this time, in the heat of it, my head bursts through the end like a mushroom battering ram. Fuck it. I keep going, get even larger. She gasps and I pound away with a rubber turtleneck around my pecker. She laughs as if insane. The rain slashes at the building like Christ receiving his flogging. Another emerald flash from another train throws animal shadows against the wall.

Then it is over, and the panting has stopped.

Wish I could stay tonight, the rain…And I live so far from here.

Some other time.

Then she is dressed. As she leaves the room she says, And you don't owe me anything.

The words hang in the air like a smile in flames.

Still lying in bed I hear her in the street climbing into the taxi beneath my window. Door slams and the cab drives away sizzling over wet pavement.

And you don't owe me anything. The words are lodged in my mind.

Probably pay for the fare by trade, I say softly to myself.

Lying in the darkness the rain cutting at the windows I envision the whole thing. They're talking it over right now. The driver's crotch is stiffening, has to reach down and tweak the material to make room. She's cooing from the backseat, touching his shoulder and nape of neck, smiling into the rearview mirror. At her place

30

he ducks the cab into some nice safe hole and climbs into the back. Do you like Thomas Mann? she says, and slips it into her mouth.

Love. Love.

JOE ON SPACEMAN

And Joe says yeah I love Spaceman, he just gets on my
nerves sometimes ya know, he's a little *crazy*, but I love
that guy man. You know why he is the way he is?
Calling himself God and all that shit? Like he was doin
the other night, right? All that Venus and space stuff?
You don't just make up that shit if you don't got a brain
ya know. I mean there has to be some intelligence there
in order to come up with the stuff he comes up with.
Rumigoes. Says the money on Mars is called rumigoes
and all the money on Mars adds up to about seven
dollars U.S. He use'ta be a colonel in the Marine Corps.
I was only a corporal. Got a big part of his brain blown
out in Korea from a mine, scotta plate in his head. Took
me out to dinner one night and told me all this stuff.
He's on pension from the federal government. Gets
twentyfourhundred a month. One time I got suspended
from here. I don't know, mouthed off ta Ron the owner
or sometin, the old queen. But anyway I was outta work
for a week and a half and I was really short on cash and
who was the first one ta offer ta help me out? Space-

32

man. He goes Joe I know what happened and I know your lifestyle here's a hundred bucks. If you need more just gimme a call, he says. The reason why he talks like he does, that space shit, at least this is what I tink, in Korea he was a prisoner of war and because he was a colonel they'd interrogate him. And ya know—well you're not a histry buff Blu but I use'ta teach histry so I know this…Those Koreans were the worst motherfuckers when it came ta torture and getting information. They'd do some tings man…Here Joe stares straight into my eyes and shakes his head with silent horror of the idea and I can feel the beam of his stare penetrate the black mirror hole of my pupils right into my cerebellum where its reflected and bounced straight to you and I'm sure you're nodding your head with sad understanding just like I am…Everything I experience I feel like you experience too, through me, because you dwell within me…Anyway Spaceman would feed'em this babble about American arsenals on Mars and space travel and shuttle crafts, drove the translators crazy tryin ta keep up with him tryin ta translate this crap into Korean to show their superiors. No one hearda this stuff back then and he'd tell'em the same shit over and over, and they began to believe it after a while. They tought America had weapons in space and were creating colonies an were gonna take Korea over. An after the shrapnel tore his brain apart this babble got kinda lodged in what was left and now he does it as a kinda like a continual defense against the world, like he feels there are spies everywhere and they're tryin ta get information out'ta him so he has'ta keep spewin this stuff. He knows it's bullshit he doesn't really believe it, but he's still a fucking colonel at heart and he feels like he has'ta protect the country. So, in a way, at least to his mind, he talks and says the tings he does for us, to save us from hostile invasion of another country.

WHACK!

Tried tricks to get me to come back, didn't ya? Sex tricks. That letter you sent where you'd drawn outlines of your breasts and open legs, body parts to the paper traced around with the pen, that drove me crazy. *My breasts are sad without you* written over your drawing of the left one. Even a place where you'd tried to make a scratch 'n sniff with some of your vaginal fluid. Alright I know I requested that one I admit, but I didn't think you'd actually do it. The spot on the paper where you put it was all wavy and dim. Circled and labeled with arrows so I wouldn't miss it. Scratched and scratched and sniffed hard at it but no scent came. Nice try though, Hon. And the illustrated anthology of erotica you sent for Christmas, got lots of mileage out of that. When I got tired of the book I cut some of the drawings out and hung them around the apartment. I like the etching in the bathroom the best, the one of the two lesbians. Woman spread on the edge of a bed, one heel digging into the mattress, stocking loosened from the garter and hanging down around her ankle, other leg dangling toes to the floor where the other woman kneels leaning her face inches over the open rose (can almost smell the salt water) and pokes her index finger oh so gently into the vulnerable exposed anus of the woman on the bed who tosses the tiny teeth of her smile at us, her fingers lightly round the horizon curve of the back of the head of the one giving her pleasure. Looks like a scene after a night on the town, maybe Paris. They look French anyway. The one kneeling on the floor still has her dress on, that's what gets me. You know how I always asked you to keep your dress on. It's open down the back and drooping off one shoulder. Side of her breast breaks partially through from the black shadow beneath her, light emerging from darkness. That's a nice touch. Bottom of the dress raised over her asshills where the fingers of the other hand of the woman on the bed tickle in the crevice. My god. You knew how to get my attention alright, a sharp *WHACK!* at the back of the cranium with the bamboo stick of the beginning word. I got the idea...Tried to get me as hot as possible so I'd want to come streaming back to your waiting arms and thighs. And yeah, how I wanted you...

Looking through an old sketchbook today I found the drawings we did of each other. First the one you did of me when I was asleep, just my face, like a death mask. I hope someone makes a plaster mold of my face when I die so they can hang my white death smile in galleries, like Keats. Then the soft portrait I did of you in quarter turn looking to the side that you said made you look like a man. It did not. And the two by candlelight you did of me later that night. Let me draw *you* for a change, you said. Nude stretched out on the bed with a hardon. I was cold. A little self-conscious too under such close scrutiny. Your eyes fixed so intently on my penis made it jump. Your drawing made it look so big and fat like a doorknob on the end. Generous of you…The other drawing is of your fist with my cock wrapped inside like a sausage hanging out of a bun. You had to keep stroking me so it'd stay hard and you wouldn't lose your model, and I'd reach for you and you'd say stop, wait, wait I almost got it, and you'd jerk me some more then suddenly stop and focus your eyes in again through the golden haze of the light coming from the candle on the floor beside the bed, long Modigliani shadows flickering all over the wall behind me and on the ceiling, and you'd say wait wait and scratch down some more lines and stroke me quickly for a couple seconds and then stop and fill in some more details and I couldn't wait I was busting all over for you. After we finally made love you went WOO! you filled me up that time! Whaddaya tryin to do embalm me with your juice?

That's right. I wanted your death in the drowning of me, in the pearly Blu Sea full of passion creatures to fill you up like Ophelia floating from this dream into the morning of the next. Wanted the fluid of me to weight you down deeper into the depths of me and hold you there forever at the bottom of my embrace. I wanted to fuck you so that you'd stay mine always in the deepest memory of your body. It's the body that never forgets…

NIGHT TRAIN AND SPACEMAN

There's a fire hydrant right outside the door of the Pay 'n Save bodega at the corner of Guerrero and 18th that Night Train uses as a stool. Sits there alone, holds out his big plastic cup to customers going in and out, cinches up his black pixie face like a gorilla fist, squishes his mouth open in a no-front-teeth-gape smile through the black grape bunch of his beard and says, Ahm juss tryin ta get me some wine…When he makes enough change he goes in, buys a quart of Night Train, pours it into his big cup that's always cradled in the crook of his arm, and goes back to his hydrant. Tonight as I round the corner at Guerrero he's sitting cradling his cup in a headlock singing *Ahm the king of the wiii-noos…Ahm the number one wiii-noo…Ahm the king of the wiii-noos…*wearing a Santa Claus hat.

*

Night upon us again like a still hairy tarantula about to lay a quick brood of intelligent children—from my seat at the end of the bar I see through the open doorway **500** CLUB reflected like a pink carnival or neon cotton candy twisted into ciphers on the side windows of a van stopped just outside at the traffic light. Light changes and the carnival spills tumbling acrobatics from the van like a sunset-colored sheath of water slipping over a fall. I am forever composing letters in my head, letters telling you everything I see and do, letters I won't write or if I do won't send because you will not accept them any longer or respond. Never believed that you're always with me, never believed that you're never out of my head or heart, never believed how much I want you next to me to touch your hand to caress your back your hair to whisper at to kiss...to make me laugh. I just want to share every little thing with you. Your eyes haunt me, hunt me like green kites. Christ why wouldn't you stay when I asked you to! Guess you couldn't accept my dream you needed to live one of your own and I ruined yours when I left. *But why did you leave me!* you said. We made plans for you to follow, remember? After I got set up. The idea all along was for you to join me here. I wasn't really leaving you, really, I was just going ahead to pave the way. But San Francisco too strange and far away for you, you didn't like it. Left after three weeks. Drove all the way out here from Illinois with your little car jammed full of your little life and you left after only three weeks. I couldn't wait to see you coming home from work. I'd run up the big flight of stairs to the apartment to you, your face looming in my brain eyes, running to you, to you...Bought two bottles of champagne and a bouquet of daisies for your first night arrival to San Francisco. Had one full bottle in me before you rang my buzzer. One bottle would be enough for the two of us, I drunkenly rationalized. Of course it wasn't. Had to come down here to the 500 after we polished that off after polishing *each other* off in bed. Your sister having just given birth to fertility-pill-fed triplets kept calling and crying to you over the phone for you to go back and be near her and her babies. *Her* babies…Shit she had those kids for your mother, because your mother wanted grandchildren, because your mother thought grandchildren would ease the boredom she felt for her own existence. I know it you know it and your sister goddamn knows it. Still you couldn't understand my contempt. And now your sister tells you she regrets marrying the man who gave her those children…Just so there's no mistake my contempt was this: pregnancy if it happens planned or not should be natural and spontaneous, never forced. Your sister forced those babies not *one* but *three* little souls to come here through miracle grow drugs when they were obviously so reluctant. Months and months of intercourse in vain. Pity… And then when she did have them she wanted to saddle you with the responsibility right along with herself, and you let her.

Love. Love.

I still use that girlie comforter the one you brought out here with you, the one we used on our own bed when we lived together. Left it for me because you

41

knew I was too poor to buy another. Girlie pink and powder blue with irises, or some kind of flower print, and a ruffle for godsake. Still can't afford a different one. Or maybe I could scrape up enough but something always stops me. Relic I'm not willing to part with yet. Some love is so delicate it can only thrive, can only *exist* in a certain time and certain place. Transplant it and the love goes into shock and turns to black wither. It wasn't your need to be away it was mine and so you could never be a part of San Francisco the way I am. I hear the ocean in your skin, you said, in your face and in your chest. Holding each other in the yellow dimness of the kitchen the night before you left to go back, knowing that I would not follow, that I belong to this place now and not to you.

San Francisco is a city of misfits. Those who seem to dry up anywhere else are somehow embraced here and flourish like germs in the mouth. This city became the other woman, the mistress, home wrecker. Never told you this but during your time here when we were in bed once and I was down doing things between your thighs it suddenly occurred to me—Chinatown! Suddenly smelled all the scents roaming the red and gold streets of Chinatown filled with fish markets that have little live blue crabs snapping and crawling anxiously over one another in dry cardboard boxes and groupers on ice with bubble eyes of death sitting out front on the sidewalks; Chinatown filled with crowded vegetable stands and steaming noisy little restaurants with shiny amber bodies of roasted ducks dangling like criminals from the neck in windows dripping strings of sugary glaze to flies (devoured one of those ducks once with bare fingers and a liter of red Gallo in the Chinese park between Clay and Washington sharing the shredded carcass with the mob of pigeons at my feet, not knowing until then that pigeons are carnivorous too), Buddha Bar loafing Sunday afternoons with beer and sake, the ancient narrow alleyways winding like a big vacant ulcerous intestine where I've stood alone against brown brick buildings eating fried chicken legs while people passed turning their heads to look at me baring my teeth in a bite; Chinatown, all the young yellow pearcheeked long-blackhaired beauties, hair like black wayward monks streaming to empty into the mountain chimes and the inert liberty of sanctuary, they shine right past you with dark splintmoon eyes as they move through the crowd running along the arms of their mothers into the long descent of young womanhood and the deaths of men's hearts…Chinatown, your pussy smelled like Chinatown, and you became the city that I love and the city became the woman that I love and in eating you I ate the city. Never showed you the vow I wrote after we proclaimed ourselves married in that intersection that time did I? What if I send it to you now? No, too late… And who do you let between your legs now I wonder? How did that vow go anyway? You know I always said I wanted to marry you on some windy weedy hill just the two of us. I told you that over and over. But can I

43

wear a pretty dress? you asked. Yes of course of course, and I'll be naked. I just don't want your parents or anybody there just us, because it's a vow only for and between us. Now doesn't that seem more natural to you? But my sister I got to have my sister there, and my mom my mom would just shit she'd never stop crying...How *did* that vow go?...Something like—Beneath...no...*Under* the witness of these clouds, this sky, whose presence is everywhere...yeah that's it...I tell you that you are the other, and together we are the same, and together we shall walk through the travel and torment and wonder of our days, not as conquerors but as loose participants in a mysterious drama that refuses to reveal the whole light of its play. In the laughing garden of ourselves it is the long journey that will carry us upward, and all the treasure we discover along the way. It is the journey we seek, and not the arrival...I guess I took our intersection interlude a bit more seriously than you did, although we both knew it was all in fun of course. Still, I meant it. But can I wear a pretty dress? Sure yes I want you to wear a pretty dress, but just us OK? We can't do that Blu. Think of the presents, the money, it would really help out. We'd need that. And I told you I have to have my family there... Jesus I miss your ey—

No no Night Train you know you're not allowed in here. I already gave you a dollar earlier. C'mon man...

Hi Joe...Ahm juss tryin ta get me a lil wine. Ah know you gamme a dollah before but I spent it huh huh

huh…Ah juss came by ta see how y'all doin ahuh huh…

No no Night Train I love ya but ya gotta go.

Night Train you know as much as you sit out there on that hydrant—

No Spaceman don't talk to him he's gotta *go!*

—the Venusians could come by and suck you up with their beams, right? You know what they do with winos like you?

No what they do huh huh huh…

They pump your stomach—

Spaceman!

—and make this kind of mush out of the contents they gather from there, add these herbs indigenous only to Venusia, right? Which is about three hundred and thirty thousand miles by earth's calculations from Venus, they don't like to be mixed up with one another—long ongoing crisis between those two. Anyway they let that stuff dry hard and crunchy—

Oh Jesus CHRIST!

—and they feed it to their cats, right? A delicacy to their cats. And their cats are very important to them, right? Practically run the place. Like to keep'em happy, right? Course their cats aren't anything like the cats we have here they're—

Night Train Night Train here, here's a couple bucks. Now get going I *mean* it!

Awright Joe now don't get mad Ahm goin now *night* e'rybody huh huh huh…Feed it to their cat huh huh

huh...*Ahm the king of the wiii—*

OFF NIGHTS

Flou-wear…Flou-wear…Flou-wear…

The voice is strange, disembodied floating down from some unknown region, from another spinning world where spiders dance for coins on sandy pathways and poodles linger at meat market windows to say prayers. I don't know what it is at first or where it's coming from.

Flou-wear…Flou-wear…Flou-wear…

What is that and what does it mean?

Looking over either shoulder and up above at the ceiling for maybe a speaker piping it in—crazy idea I know but I have no idea what it could be, enveloping sound yet so distant—looking around I see only hurried pushing faces crowding around me with hard self-preserving mouths and eyes and mustaches and sunglasses, people carrying briefcases umbrellas wearing backpacks overcoats pushing bicycles all clustering and pressing me in like I'm the little raw piece of fish center of a sushi roll and they're the rice sticking to me in the round. 16th and Mission BART station. Coming back from Oakland where I spent the morning wandering the marina of Jack London Square. New *Barnes & Noble* conducting interviews over there. Out of work for more than a month now, getting desperate, running the savings into the ground. But I'm optimistic. Sometimes when you stand and wait long enough in one spot opportunity falls right on your head and another shit job comes along to eat you up like the last. Didn't even bother handing my application in, left it on the table where I'd filled it out. Took one look at the huge line pythoning waiting to hand in their apps and sell themselves to the smug judge panel of suit and tieds (which I can never do, I open my mouth and the only thing that comes out is the truth, so they don't want me) and said *shit to this!* I could see the disaster of the interview stretching ahead like a bloody corpse across a highway. Blu Moor, that's an interesting name, one of them would say, probably the bald pudgy one with glasses in the brown suit, and then the false smile slowly bubbles from the miasma within to the surface of my lips forcing me to press back the gag in my throat lodged there by the same words I've heard all my life about my name coming at me yet again—always the same comment. And then, when the fake smiles slide away all around: Well now Mr. Moor, we see here you've had a number of jobs and none of them for very long, what makes you think you're a good candidate for position with our prestig-ious company at its newest outlet? Get up without a word and walk out, visions of skulking back in the night and putting a torch to the prestige of their newest outlet. I make a good fire! I'd chuckle to myself, walk-ing away as the flames mountain behind me over my shoulder.

Headed back home after strolling my fill of the docks, of course. Why waste a trip to see new things. Never get to Oakland much—never much want to. Wondered a long time over the log cabin they have as a monument in the Square to Jack London that ole Jack supposedly lived in in Alaska. Rope cot, dirt floor carpeted with pennies and dimes and nickels people'd tossed in there through the bars caging the entrance like the thing was a wishing well (induce some adventure into their lives by buying it off, no risk of loss that way), dusty lantern on the wall, and outside grass and tall weeds shooting up on the sod roof needing a hair-cut. Thought of howling crisp bites of wind and wool and flying swirls of snow and bearded warm story gab-bing fires with beans gobbled out of small tins, tired muscles, twinkling dreams. The weak and fearful are al-ways raising monuments to the strong. It's vicarious-ness, vapid vampirism that says thanks for coming we've enjoyed sucking on your life but we can't follow. No more monuments, please. Cheapens the whole af-fair. Emulation is best. Does pain produce art or does art produce pain? Yes. No. Neither. Both. The pain is there regardless. The art, as always, is a matter of opin-ion.

Flou-wear…Flou-wear…

The faces as I look tell me nothing, as if they don't

hear don't care don't wonder even and we all keep moving herding toward the ticket gates to get back up into the light of the racing world (in the underground Time takes a big shot of morphine and slows way down to where it seems you're barely breathing and you feel all snug like you're curled back up in your mama's bed belly and you pull the watery blankets up to your chin to peacefully nap and the world just takes a hike for a while, doesn't exist almost, till you get back up top and the clock's a nasty old cokehead again blabbering away and prodding you along to its insane amphetamine drum beat solo orchestra demanding your constant attention and draining your energies precious and personal energies that you'd rather use up on yourself) and just as I take my turn through the gate like a good cattle member...Flou-wear...Flou-wear...I see the faces parting and falling away heading toward the escalator and then the brown face the brown hand, pink roses wrapped in cellophane offered stretched-out from the hand, big white plastic bucket on the floor housing dozens more roses...Flou-wear...Flou-wear...and the mystery's solved...If you were here I'd buy you one, maybe. Never been too good at that. Always seemed too obvious and easy to really mean anything unless you've grown the flowers yourself or picked them from some secret wild patch that only you know about (Remember the wild tiger lilies I picked for you that summer? I could almost swear no one else knew of them, or if they did they never picked them. Probably too odd a place, no one thought of going there to gather flowers. They grew deep in the train yard and bloomed only in mid July. Had to walk along the tracks for some ways till I got to the spot. And heading back to my car I'd keep looking at the orange exploding lily mouths sprouting now from my fist like strange tongues spotted with brown fever and I'd smile knowing, *hoping* they'd make you smile.) then you're participating in the beauty if only in a contrived and small way; then there's true sincerity behind the gesture…Always been amazed though that women even fall for such a graphic ploy… My head always gets in the way…

And I know this man, at least I've seen him before at the 500 Club. Comes in to drink Budweiser and play pinball, his bucket of roses waiting on the stone mantel seat of the fireplace beside him as he plays. They can wait. He's been pushing those cocksucking flowers all over the hot Mission streets now they can just wait in their water while he waters himself…Goddammit Santa Maria turn way your head while I get borracho and mingle with de gueros and make a muchacha or dos. I never ask to enter de inferno of diss warld, now go lay your petal peddling on someone else's tired shouldars. I'm *seek!* Seek of all diss *hurry!* No one buys anyway. Dese fat Americanos have no need for de beauty I offar, and at a huge bargain too. What do dey care? I just want to *eeeat* to drink my Bud*weiii*ser and screw a muchacha, or maybe a muchacho *dressed* as a muchacha I don't care anymore, just so I get my dry leettle stem into someding moiss and my arms around some lahv…

I actually did see him one time with a very unattractive man in drag, Hispanic too, long goldenorange ponytail. They were sitting in one of the round booths at the 500, a booth like Al Capone must've sat and drank in in Chicago with his cigar and guns and floozies all attentive and doting, rounds of martinis to flush out the gullet. Same booth design like from that era. And just like Al Capone all chubby and proud and feeling in control the Mexican was sprawling with arm over back of booth around his companion, his big belly puffing out under the table, heels of his cowboy boots spread out teetering on their back edges on the carpet, relaxed, feeling pleased with himself, like he'd just picked this creature up at another bar (Esta Noches perhaps on 16th, the Latino drag bar) where he'd stopped to push his flowers and drain another Bud, and seeing her sitting alone perhaps offered a rose, at which she may have batted her long fake eyelashes and said, Si por favor! Gracias! Now what can I offor you? And he knew he had this one sewed-up. Come weeth me, he may have responded, I show you place, you never been…And so now he's sitting there in the 500 Club, his dubious woman on one side and his bucket of roses on the other beside him on the seat, feeling his masculinity surging with a thousand Mexican mustaches like hairy butterflies tickling in his heart and loins and his testicles jumping around and shaking in his jeans like maracas because he knows tonight all the men can see that he's got some, no pinball tonight, tonight *real* ball, flesh mono a mono…No need tonight for holes made for steel I got a rose hole to fill a*rriii*baaaaa!

But maybe he didn't know he had a drag queen. Maybe he thought he had the real soft fitting stuff. Possible. Experience counts for nothing when enough desperation or fatigue sets in, makes you overlook the obvious. Even Joe unbelievably one night missed an easy one and this one had biceps to gag a water buffalo, wig like Ray Bulger's Scarecrow-stuffing-guts tossed out of him by flying monkeys. Unbelievable because Joe usually has an eye that cuts right to the bone, capable of sizing up the mood of the bar and the character of the customers at a single glance when he's on, even when he's swamped. He knows who's fucked up and who could be trouble and even prevents it in most cases before trouble actually occurs while simultaneously maintaining control of the whole place and keeping everybody happy getting their drinks. Truly the best bartender I've ever seen. But too many late nights with too much scotch and too little sleep will take its toll, and this one night she…Well it went like this:

I'm sitting at the bar, it's pretty full, and in through the door she comes. Spot her before anyone else because I'm seated at the corner nearest the door and happen to be gazing that way when she enters—wig in wiry disarray and a bit crooked, heavy-handed makeup, big shoulders no hips, powder blue silk dress, painted

Bette Davis mouth. Walks up to the bar sits down. Joe comes over and leans in like he does in that sly way he has, lights a cigarette, slants his eyes sideways at her as he releases the smoke, and I think *oh no he's about to make a play!* But no, he's just studying her with expert bartender eye, sees she's intoxicated already, so when she says tequi'a Joe says no I'm sorry I can't serve you, you've had enough already. But she's deaf, which I pick up on right away. It's in the way she said tequila without the L—tequi'a. Unmistakable deaf voice. The mechanics of certain sounds like Ls and Cs and Js most often elude the deaf tongue. But Joe misses this fact too it turns out, or perhaps mistakes it as proof of his assessment, and I see that it's one of his off nights. She grabs his hand. 'Ome on...tequi'a...But Joe keeps refusing politely, shaking his head and looking around at the rest of the bar, blowing streams of smoke, even smiling a bit, jerking his chin like he does. She keeps pleading though and won't let go of his hand. 'Ome on! she says...Being respectful of women for the most part, and customers generally, Joe patiently waits for the hand to be removed while taking a sip of scotch with his free hand and ignoring her for other orders. But she has a grip like a truck driver and refuses to release him. Finally Joe gets sick of it and scrunches up his face and grits his teeth and leans an elbow down on the bar and says right in her clown face real low and threatening will you get the fuck outta here! You're not getting served now get out!...Look around, no one wants you in here, you're not gonna get anyting (meaning she's not gonna get laid anyway) now get out before I bash your head!...She just keeps hold and stares pathetically up at him with teary eyes, skyblue eyeshadow smeared with moisture. Guy at the stool next to her goes he said get out, now let go! and reaches to peel her hand away while Joe tries to jerk his back. But she holds tight pleading for the life nectar just out of reach at the inner lip of the bar, bicep and shoulder muscle bulging from her sleeveless dress. Suddenly she slugs the guy next to her across the back. Hey *hey!* he goes. Then Joe goes, rather softly, hey now don't go hitting other customers! That's when I realize Jesus Christ they actually think it's a real woman! A male can't get away with throwing punches in a bar (and she hit that guy pretty hard) without being shown the grain intricacies of the door up-close.

Still she has hold of Joe. 'Ome on! 'Ome on! And he says whatsamatter you fuckin deaf! Get the fuck out! he says yanking his hand away finally moving away to take care of other customers and that's that, final word on the subject. She can sit there and sob her ratty head off for all he cares (she's hiding her face in her hands and rocking back and forth on her stool) but she is not going to get his attention.

For a few minutes everyone forgets about it and turns back to their drinks and to their talk or their thoughts when suddenly SMASH! Something shatters against the door and glass sprays and everyone jumps in their seats and turns their heads. And there in the middle of that frozen moment she cuts across the floor, slugging another guy on the way across the chest saying 'on't be dawty! (don't be dirty!). The guy clutches his chest in amazed smiling wonder as his mouth forms a slow silent ouow...

Joe grabs the club from beneath the bar and makes to run out after her with murder wings dive bombing in his eyes but Blatherton, a journalist for the Independent Newspaper, stops him. Cooler head, Blatherton's gonna take care of this himself so no one gets hurt or in jail, takes hold of the crazy lady's elbow and gently escorts her to the door almost cooing at her. Alright that's enough, he says, good night miss. As she quietly exits through the threshold back into the night Blatherton closes the door after her saying good riddance miss, and saunters back to his drink with a little pleased-with-himself smile, all so calmly and collectedly. Ignorant fucking diplomat.

What was that she trew an ashtray? That coulda really hurt someone. Dirty bitch! I shoulda fuckin clubbed'er!

At this I felt compelled to clue them in. Couldn't believe Joe still had no idea.

OOOH! He laughs. I *tought* she had a pretty good grip tss-ss-ss-sss...

I don't buy a rose as I pass the Mexican but smile but I'm not buying and the Mexican doesn't know who the fuck I am so he doesn't smile back.

As I ascend to the top of the escalator into the sun tearing sneakily away at the city like the infiltration of a criminal's fingers a new voice assaults from a bullhorn ...Jew know why? the voice asks. Cuz look around jew—drugs, homeless...The horn dangles from a leather strap slung over a man's shoulder pointing behind him at his hip as he speaks into a handheld microphone. The man's face is dark brown and he wears a white long-sleeved shirt bottoned to the throat. As I pass he swings his back to me and suddenly I'm adrift in the middle of the heavy electric current blasting out a hot stream of words. My pant leg compresses swiftly against my shin...And Jesus sees jew...He knows... And he's waiting for jew to open jorself to heem jew know why?...Cuz he lahvs jew...Finally I crawl free from the current and start heading up 16th through the solicitations—Coca, Chiva—Outfiiits—as Red Man flashes by. In the burning sun his face is an overripe tomato. He's got a new variation on today, wearing a long striped skirt and a black blazer, black felt hat. I turn and look back at him as he walks on—arms out flitting delicately at his sides as if floating over the pavement, as if there were no need for his feet at all, no connection between himself and the street he passes above. Happy nut. I'm jealous.

RED BRA AND PANTIES

Gin—poet's song, hot menstrual flow, eagle's claw—
maybe I should get dreadlocks…Nah I'd hate myself.
White man robbing another culture yet once more. 30
closing in. Hair thinning into a V. Bald motherfucker
you are one bald motherfucker tell myself that every
time I look into the mirror and make snarling dog faces
at the glass to scare the hair into staying. Useless
though it's not afraid of me and has a mind and destiny
of its own to follow. How can I get girls with no hair, or
worse moldy hair. It's not that bad yet and still do alright. That's it keep that I'm OK you're OK crap going
positive energy think thin think thin think thin my eyes
…Why do people love my eyes so much? Big blue and
when they're red like now makes the blue pop even
more intensely. Compliment of colors. Push and pull of
pigments placed. I can't help it I like sounds. And
colors too. I smash them together and they come out
word paint. But there's darkness under my eyes. My
mouth moves funny when I talk, one side higher than
the other. When you got tipsy and were telling stories

your mouth always got way crooked to the left, but it's funny only when you were drinking otherwise it was straight normal. Mine's a little crooked all the time. Always had that darkness under there, my eyes, the color of iron almost, but maybe my lashes are so long they make canopies and hide that iron in cool articulated shade so people don't see it in the dimness of bars or… bars…Jawline not too bad broad and strong, stubble of beard even and full emphasizing certain curves and the red meat of my lips…Blue eyes full of sad. Maybe it's the blue against dark hair that gets'em, always a stunning combo I know I like it in women, though I prefer brown eyes brown hair. But preference means nothing I take what comes to me. The other night, sitting next to me twirling the straw in her drink: You have nice hands, she said, I like men's hands, and took my right one from the bar and held it. Her palms were warm and soft. Overweight but she was very tight and gave some of the best head I've ever had. Came back from the shower in the morning and the note on the bed said *Last night was wonderful, so was this morning. Call me.* Threw it away. I'm such an easy pickup I really have to watch that. Stretch marks on her breasts belly and thighs like she'd been jumbo once but now has slimmed down though still a ways to go and the weight has left its irrevocable impressions upon the flesh. But I can't call anything about myself stunning…Then why can you never refrain from looking in a mirror? Why do you stand staring at yourself in the mirror now talking into your own eyes holed up in Joe's bathroom while Tony screws a girl hogtied with a leather belt in the living room? She kept showing us her underwear, red bra and panties, pronounces her Ss like ssch, sound coming from the cheeks from the back of the throat around the side of the molars like hissing over the back of the tongue like say stool would be sschtool. Monique disgusted left the room to sleep in Joe's empty bed and Tony took his belt off looped it tight around the girl's wrists buried his face in her white blouse with his hat still on waved me over and I sat poised to feast, watched his big fingers creep under her skirt and dig at her panties, and she looked good, but somehow I couldn't do it. So came in here and stand looking at myself waiting for obscure insights and wisdom that won't come. But why do I do this always run to the mirror? Guess because I suspect I might be handsome but I'm not quite convinced so have to keep looking to check but the ambiguousness never lifts and I had nowhere else to go Monique in the bedroom Tony and the girl in the living room I needed solitude just a moment alone with myself please I'm drunk and I don't want to go home yet must be 3:30 and there's nothing outside this apartment but lonesome and nothing in this apartment but lonesome…I always wanted a brilliant life. I'm not easily contented like most…You said to me once Blu you're unstable too romantic you don't live in reality you don't even *see* reality. Oh my sweet little pumpkin cakes I do I certainly do but I suspend myself just below it like a turtle hangs just beneath the water's surface and only pokes its nose up through to get air like your cute little turtle's nose softly curving downward I love that nose of yours so unique. I float just beneath the surface of reality so that I can see through it. Don't you know how I work by now? Keeps the child kicking in me, I need that. And I have not had a lover since you and do I want one? No. Yes certainly. See that's the trouble mixed signals. It's all such a distraction. And am I really in love with you or am I just scared? My eyes wander perpetually. But I can stop that I know I could. Well maybe probably not stop but I could ignore it. Compromise? Certainly but you do that to retain the single support system. You do that to protect the unity precious between two people. Such a rare animal unity not everyone finds it that's why when you do it's worth fighting for. All the letters I sent you, they were a fight. And not a word in return. Unity, that's what I miss. Floating along out here like a— what'd Baudelaire call it?—widowed soul. I miss our unity. I'm too light, worn thin from the inside out. I'm drifting unraveling into the strong fade. There was a time when that's all I sought, the lightness, to float above the stink, to soar unbound. Now I'm too light. Now I want to take on weight come down a little. I'm too high. Grab hold of me baby, catch me in your tight woven goddess hands again and stop my disappearance. Courage and strength could conquer love…I don't think I want to be that brave. Unstable? Financially. Unstable? Yes darling you're right, I am unstable. The dead are no fun. They see too much but can say very little and only want more more of everything. Swallow invisibility and wait to lie back down. Look at the pores on my nose! *Yeeeesh!* As the long temple road opens to slumber, and the night invites a reckless grin still with hunger, and cold, still aching at the wait, we reach deeper into doubt and the faithless kingd—

Blu is that you?

Monique bursts through the door wearing only a white tshirt. And white sox.

Thought so, she says. Thought I heard you in here.

Goldenbrown long smooth bird legs leap at the eye. So proud of those legs thinks they're so hot shows them off whenever possible wears short short cutoffs on a regular basis. Too skinny if you ask me. Fuzzy black tip of the triangle peeks from the bottom of her shirt.

You can come in here and sleep with me if you want, Monique says.

In bed we are both naked but stay on our own sides. Moaning and thumping come through the wall from the living room. Oh are we gonna have to listen to that all night? Monique whines. I smile in the dark and drift off to sleep. Penis pulses a few times trying to perk me up but soon forgets about it and goes to sleep too.

*

Funny what a strong taste for drink and little money and quite a bit of curiosity and a friendly neighborhood dive will bring you. Tony poured Jack Daniel's into the empty Budweiser bottle and when it was full did the same with another bottle only this time filled it with gin. He pulled the pouring spouts from the mouths of two empty booze bottles (rubber stoppers with curved metal tubes sticking out of them like something from chemistry class), capped the two booze-filled beer bottles with these, then put them into the six pack holder with the other four bottles of beer. The girl had been waiting all night for him to close. Pretty, but big teeth and overbite I'd be afraid to put it in there lose two layers of skin. There seems always to be a girl hanging around the 500 waiting for Tony to close. And when there isn't there's always his girlfriend to go to. Love. Love. Monique had mentioned something earlier about Joe being gone up in Hercules visiting his ex-wife and she had the keys to his apartment, taking care of the place for a few days while he's away, and why don't we stop by later? And now that Tony'd counted his drawer and made preparations, Jack for him gin for me beer for whoever wanted it, we headed across the street to Joe's and Monique who was waiting.

She'd cooked earlier and there was leftover lasagna. Tony and I got rid of that in front of the tv with our drinks. The girls chatted in the kitchen drinking beer. And outside across the street that big cocktail glass sign darkened, all the electric life colors cut out of it, scooping up the night now in a dark monkish embrace instead of burning through it like a tireless guide. Almost made me sad to see that sign dead in the dark like that, like it had given up finally, shrugged its shoulders in a what's-the-use shrug and fired a bullet into its brain. But I knew it was only sleeping and was still alive the way Truth still exists even though there may be no one to receive it. Tony and I sat quietly. We never say much to each other anyway. Ours is an osmotic relationship. I have trouble with bullshit and he has trouble with sincerity but since this is understood there isn't any tension between us and usually just let each other be. And here it wasn't any different, the occasional grunt and snort at the tv and the slurping of a drink serving as our most pronounced mode of communication. Tony writes too, and I don't know what it is about me but other writers often seem to sniff me out and pin point me as something of their kin. Tony did this. One of the very first times I was in the 500 Club and he was bartending he came up to me, had hardly said a word to him, leaned each hand on a tap handle and drummed his fat fingers and said so what do you do?—a wary look of recognition almost like an accusation glinting from behind his eyes. And I said what do I do to make money or what do I really do? (because that question always needs clarification, at least at this stage, and probably always will). And he said what do you do that satisfies you personally? And when I responded that I write he smirked and nodded and said thought so, and then it was the inevitable question and answer and parry and thrust routine that goes along with this type of first meeting which I couldn't give a shit about (Paul Klee's etching *Two Men Meet Both Supposing The Other Of Higher Rank* always comes to mind in these situations, two naked men half-bent dangling long arms like apes sniffing round each other, surmising and feeling each other out—Klee was so succinct with his titles like a Jack the Ripper surgeon cutting straight to the heart of the ghost) because whenever asked which writers I admire they're most often shot down and jeered at anyway for one reason or another. Not academic enough so therefore not serious or valid, or they're a dinosaur so insignificant, or oh that guy was just a speed freak pervert couldn't write for shit ya ever heard of...? And they feel compelled to lay some names on me who are absolutely *the* shit, no doubt about it they know how to write and only they are worthy artists to study, the others trite waste of time. S'why I genuinely dislike most writers, jeering and dogmatic baboons generally, and I'm not totally excluding myself. They forget all about the subjectivity of their art. I don't care what people read or don't read. I'm in this for myself. The fucks should know better. I'd slaughter them with a swipe of my paw if I didn't want to have to lick and bite the dried blood out from beneath my nails later. Whenever I'm asked now I deny it. No, I'm no writer— you're mistaken.

So there is a tacit agreement between Tony and myself not to discuss writing and without that, aside from the booze, there's very little connection. And I'd just about finished my beer bottle of gin and the panties were red they certainly were and still were every time she threw back her skirt to show us and the bra we could see through the thin white gauze of her blouse was red too, mmhmm a match, that's right darlin. I sschpent fifteen minutessche tonight trying to desschide which underwear to put on. And *oh my god* Monique didn't feel like competing with that high school girlie fuck me crap and who could blame her and went to bed.

*

Wake to Monique bucking her rump against me like a cat. What's this? I'd gotten a hardon during sleep and she must have come up against it (we're lying spoon style), turned her on. Takes me a few seconds to shake the numbness from my brain and realize but when I do I grab her hip and hump her ass and she takes my hand and places it on her breast and reaches back to take hold of me and jerks up and down, up, down, up down, and I turn her over and stagger to my knees and crouch like a lion at the river's skirt for a drink and split the foliage with my hands and lap lap lap thirsty and when I go to put it in she says not without a rubber I told you that and gets kinda mad but I swear I didn't hear a goddamn thing about a stinking rubber and so shrug and go back to sleep.

THE WISDOM OF COCKROACHES

There's a cockroach on my kitchen floor struggling on its back to regain its feet. Seems like I've been sitting here at the table watching it for hours but I know that's not so. Daytime plays tricks on me, moves along with legs made of lead like anchors allowing minutes to elongate themselves into tunnels of infinity. Night, night floats by like caustic bliss.

Hard afternoon light squeezes in through the steel grating that covers the kitchen window and the room's white walls are flooded dull pale and bright. The flesh that covers the day is rotten. Just once I wish night would stay, reign supreme. Never come morning, and all the stink forgotten.

I could lift my foot and crush the roach's guts out. It's like a human sacrifice, a body languishing over an altar with its chest thrust outward waiting for me to plunge the blade and deflate the life billowing in the lungs and heart.

*

Insane creature running wildly Chagall upside down,

running frantically yet motionless like in a bad dream, as if expecting my foot to come down on it at any instant. Wonder if it thinks it's in a nightmare? I bend down and look more closely. Twitching hairfine feelers, armor plating of its sides. Flipped over Volks Wagon with spinning wheels. I can almost read its tiny insect mind and hear the gentle thunder raging in its tiny insect heart racing with fright. It's crazy with fear and vulnerability. Legs beat electrically. It'll die all on its own of it does not turn over soon, of heart attack.

*

Utterly helpless. Almost begs me now to put it out of its misery. It can't stand the cruel terror and suspense. I am lord over it. I decide its fate. I'm toying with it the way a cat toys with its kill. Give it a chance. I kick it. Slides across the floor. Didn't help still can't get its legs. Kick it back with the other foot. I play hockey with it. I'm sitting in my kitchen playing hockey with a cockroach on the floor, toying with it like a cat, internally cursing the day on fire, and I wonder why it is I cannot feel anything.

*

The legs weave me into a kind of trance. I am no longer here. I am a very small blue bubble somewhere in the depths of inner space, in the garden of heaven. I do not exist but I am thoroughly alive. Suddenly I am looking down the long brown corrugation of my belly at the nest of legs waving tantrums in the air, *my* legs; looking down the oblong pill of my body stretching like an unappetizing feast along the altar of sacrifice. My head is stuffed with silent echoing screams.

Sacrifice. The night I left for San Francisco is a scar on my memory; like a scratch on a record my needle keeps getting snagged in the gash. On the way to the bus station from the restaurant where we had our good-bye dinner you pulled the car over along the curb of some darkened street among some other parked cars to have one more goodbye bang. So sudden it surprised me a little. Hurry up you get those pants down, you said. Sure sure…The car rocked gently in the darkness, you straddling my lap. A guy with a little black dog on the sidewalk noticed the soft undulation of the car, did you see him? Paused briefly at our window knowing, then continued on with his dog.

Wet spring night. No stars shown in the sky's patchy countenance only ominous dark blue cotton rolls blowing toward the moon of summer. I remember watching those clouds slowly drift across the windshield as you pumped over me. Streets glistened and sidewalks were spattered maroon, thick with fallen new buds of trees blown off from the unrelenting rainstorms of cherub-faced Illinois April. Going away and maybe never see you again, both thinking it, although the plan is for you to join me—at least that was the plan in *my* mind— somehow though…somehow we both sense this is the end…I was going away and I was already missing your big green Saharalike eyes, that is, eyes like those of some soothsayer desert princess aflame wide at the fire with childlike silent beating horseleg visions racing round your skull tender—already I was missing all the humor you saved for me within yourself in case I found my way out of the mind labyrinth alive and go to you finally stripped and purified and no longer broodingly with angst for myself, my life...You could always make me laugh, oldman stoneface me, you could always get a smile to come like springtime decimating icy snow...I was going away and we could hardly speak or look at each other, only stare off into the distant silence of our own separate open landscapes and wonder, and remember...

I'll go to her one day as to the one and only church, I told myself, and be saved...Now you are gone, for good...And the agony is I feel I am almost ready for that church but know its doors are no longer open to me—salvation hidden away forever inside...

And the face of you as I stepped onto that Greyhound and turned to look back one last quick time into your eyes, one last mean moment that lasted only seconds in actual time but in the time of the heart it was the size of a year, a little sickly smile on both our mouths, a smile full of apologies on my part and pain and distant hope for you, for *us* in the future, and bashful selfishness, and on yours a smile of weakening strength that said I will not cry I will not cry, then a little quiver shook your chin, but just a little one, almost imperceptible...And there in that tortured blur of Time was the sound of two shattering hearts like glaciers splintering and dropping away in a thunderous melt that deafened and tore the universe asunder but could not be heard by a single solitary soul but for two small and sad humans parting awkwardly in the damp night at the steps of an impatient bus. Long slow purple funeral train of a love, passing, and no one there to even bow his head.

Alone in my dark seat tears were rivers wriggling all over my face like a lost map as the bus lumbered and bumped out of that town, the town of my earthly growth but which strangely never felt like home. And as I looked out the window as the bus slowly went the night and the buildings as they rolled by swam in my eyes, swam with me into the west, gone. And what had happened? Had you even existed, or was the warm love happiness you brought and this rose bleed agony both empty spaces of the same unequal fevered dream? Gone, and what have I done, and what am I chasing and what am I fleeing to and what do I want to transpire and who the hell do I think I am anyway to kick love away? Someone who knows himself well enough to recognize that if he does not leave, if he does nothing to bring himself into being there will *be* no being, human or otherwise, only a puddle, only a tepid wasting puddle wishing for evaporation.

I reached into my jacket and brought out the envelope you had given me over dinner with instructions not to look until I was on the bus. It was even written on the back of the envelope: OPEN AFTER YOU

LEAVE BUS STATION! Why were you so afraid for me to look before? I turned on the overhead light wiped my eyes opened the envelope and read the card that was tucked away inside. It was printed neatly all in capital letters in black ink.

DEAREST BLU—
PLEASE UNDERSTAND WHEN I SAY I WANT YOU TO DO WHAT'S RIGHT FOR YOU AND NOT TO WORRY ABOUT MY LOYALTY TO YOU. I COULD NEVER WANT OR DESIRE ANYONE BUT *YOU* WHILE WE'RE APART. I WANT YOU TO CONCEN- TRATE ON YOUR ART AND FINDING IN- NER PEACE. I'LL LOVE YOU ALWAYS AND THINK OF YOU COMPULSIVELY AND OB- SESSIVELY. (NOT THAT I DIDN'T DO THAT WHEN YOU WERE HERE, BUT MY LOVE AND LONELINESS WILL BE HEIGHTENED WHEN YOU'RE GONE.) I WILL ALWAYS BE HERE IF YOU WANT TO CALL TO TALK OR MAYBE JUST TO NOT TALK BUT ONLY LISTEN TO EACH OTHER'S BREATHING. IT HURTS ME TO HAVE TO WRITE THIS. NOT THAT I'M SAD BECAUSE YOU'RE LEAVING AND I'M NOT, BUT THAT YOU ARE FOL- LOWING YOUR HEART AND SOUL AND I'M JUST WORKING. NOT LISTENING TO MY- SELF BUT ONLY TO OTHERS' ADVICE. BE

TRUE TO YOURSELF AND TO YOUR ART. I
LOVE YOU BUDDY, AND WILL MISS YOU
DEEPLY.

It was signed with that characteristic heart you'd
draw at the end of each letter. My hand mopped my
face.

For this you are gone, accumulation of words like a
child composed of thousands of black ants; for life and
art and birth you are gone. And there are many kinds of
torture, I know. Many kinds of dry idle worship and in-
ward flapping sheets that tear a man to rags and leaves
him wondering and wandering but art, art is the most
sullen knife-toothed monster of them all because you
don't know what it is and why you're pursuing it with
such self-exposed venom. It's a ghost in a black closet
with a torn see-through veil of a smokedripping shroud.
But why did you leave me! you screamed to me over the
phone in frustration. Certainly didn't leave to leave you,
I promise that forever. But how could I explain then
that I left to fuck a sick ghost of a shroud in a closet
instead of your warm body in our bed?

Ah art's a ghost you're a ghost I'm a ghost. My entire life consists of stalking apparitions and little more. I
didn't know how to explain that I left for self-trans-
formation; left for a place where I could let myself slide
from myself into a cool new pond of fresh skin and
reemerge with a proclamation, a triumphant shout of
SELF!—that I am finally my own creature and no one

has any reins attached to my jowls. Had to sacrifice myself in order to save myself.

Sacrifice—listen…hear the thick sick sound of sacrifice dripping from a punctured love gobs of blood dropping small explosions upon the marble…

*

Without even knowing what I'm doing, back in my chair at the table, back in the flesh in which I was born, I reach down and help the roach over with my finger. It crawls away easily beneath the stove as if nothing had ever happened; crawls away from the unsure terror of its upside down moment into the easy freedom of its right-side up moment without a care or a scurry. Or a backward glance.

Out loud I say to no one: Never underestimate the wisdom of cockroaches.

SPEAKING IN BRAILLE

And is there a page missin or somethin? Your first sentence starts with the word *And*? *And the mad rush of the blue blurry night...*? Sounds like somethin's happened before this, Blatherton says. Sounds like we're being left outta somethin.

Awright look, Blatherton continues, you don't start a book with the word *And.* Look...Alright...Look, he says, searching for words...OK, he says finally, the first sentence of a book scottabe a gripper, it's gotta get the reader's intrest otherwise he's just gonna put it back on the rack and move on. You didn't get me till all the way down here in the middle of the paragraph with this *No those wolves got us pretty good, we've had it awright*...Now *there's* your first line! You got my attention with that. But...Look, as they say in the newspaper business you've buried your *lead.* You should start with this line down here—*No those wolves got us...*—and go on from there. Forget about all this stuff up here...He flutters his hand over the top of the page. Awright, that's the first thing I'd tell ya. Now—*...blue blurry* *night…*Can the night be blue? he asks, lowering the pages to the surface of the bar with a far-off thoughtful rhetorical blankness in his eyes. I look at him.

I've been quiet the whole time, haven't said a word while Blatherton has gone over the manuscript, rambling on and on, picking at anything that appears to his dull mind to be a loose thread. I let him talk, hoping he'd talk himself into some cohesion finally, into some idea of what I was trying to do. If he just reads far enough, I told myself, if I just let him be to discover it on his own without my saying anything I'll get a more accurate and honest opinion. But this…this *can the night be blue?* shit! I know I've made a big stupid mistake. The stuff needs a wider more tender eye. I'm never doing this again…*What!* finally I say. You're telling me you've never seen a blue night? A blue sky at night?

No, he says. I haven't. It's black. Or *inky*. I've never seen a blue night.

Oh my god this guy's an idiot a fucking *idiot* I wish you could hear this guy why did I show him these pages *I'm* an idiot! Newspaper man, not a creative hair on his stinking body…

…*Blue blurry night*, he reads, *swirling along our car's windows and licking at us with its wind only adds to the terror…*—What terror? Blatherton says. I don't feel any terror.

He's trapped in the back of a speeding car, I say, his father's driving and his mother's sitting up there too, and they're about to fly off the side of a cliff...You've read at least that far, right? It's only the next page... And you don't feel that horror?

No, he says, I don't. Lenny can we have a couple more? Scotch and soda, and give Blu—what's that Blu?—gin and *tonic* please!

I don't usually come to the 500 during the afternoon but Random House sent its rejection slip today and there was nothing left for me to do. The latest attempt to publish the book I finished just before leaving for San Francisco; the latest failure in San Francisco.

Lenny's the skinny Scotsman who tends bar in the day. He brings the drinks and says to me with dingy blue eyes poking over his glasses (does that whenever he wants to make sure his point gets across, lets his spectacles slide down the slope of his nose to the tip and stares at you over the top of the lenses, his knobby knuckles pressed to his thin white-aproned hips) Lenny says to me, Coople moor a doze an yuulll be speckin in *brlaille!* Tony sitting a few stools down from my right reading the newspaper waiting for his shift to start (it's almost switch over time) lets a short laugh snore through his nose. I toss a look over at him but his attention's forced down at his paper. Blatherton came in when it was just me and Lenny in the place. Saw the manila envelope and asked about it. I don't know, I let him look out of vulnerability I guess. I needed a finger to help me over off my back. Figured a few words from a guy who actually makes a living off of words couldn't hurt. Forgot for a moment that writing and what I do are two totally separate animals. Decline in the evolution has forced them to separate as if a hose had been trained upon them.

I drag my eyes from Tony back to Blatherton. I'm gonna say this once, I say loud enough for everyone to hear (don't Blu don't!), because I think I'm only *able* to say it once right now. The first page is a recount of a dream wherein the protagonist has regressed back to a child's perspective (oh Jesus Blu don't do this don't do this just stop now just *stop!*) that's why its tone seems so wondrous or naïve. And by the way it begins with *And* because you're right, something *has* happened before that, more of the dream but more than that even an entire *life* has happened, see? The word *And* is meant to imply that without having to *say* it. Anyway…uh… where was I, shit…Uh yeah (don't, *don't!*)…that whole dream sequence states metaphorically the entire theme of the book. If you'd bother looking at the other thirty pages there taken from various parts of the manuscript you'd understand a little better instead of spending a half a fucking hour picking over the first fucking page. We've barely gotten off the first paragraph for godsake and we've been talking about this for *half an hour!* That first part's important *all of it* because like I said it states metaphorically the major theme of the book, and that is…I take a breath, Jesus Christ why am I saying this shit shut up Blu just *shut up!*…It's like this, I say, once you've realized fully the inevitability of death, the very first time I mean, when the idea finally sinks in and you realize that one day you are going to die and be gone for good—*you!*—when that hits you once and for all it's like being trapped helplessly in a speeding car that only increases its speed toward the end while you frantically search for ways to defeat that end, or at least go kicking and screaming. The faster the car goes the more unreal and unattainable life seems, so you cling to it even more to try to find some…uh…substanti…uh substanti*a*lity. And you have no idea what the hell I'm talkin about cuz you haven't read the goddamn thing and neither did Random House. And I don't think you'd get it even if you *did* read it. Just give the fucker back OK? Just give it back…I reach for the pages but Blatherton goes no no lemme take it home and look it over another time. I always read before I go to bed, he says, I'll look at it then, awright? But, look, I gotta go right now. He puts the pages back inside the envelope and stuffs the envelope inside his leather satchel. Then he lifts his drink, sucks it all in till the ice rattles against the glass, puts the glass back on the bar and gets off his stool. I'll get it back to ya I promise Blu. Lemme look it over when I have more time and I'll get it back to ya. Shakes my hand. See ya Lenny, have a good evening. Tony, take it easy. And with that Blatherton's out the door. And I am nauseous with self-exposure and my skin crawls at the very small thought of myself.

That's the last you'll see a *that*, Tony laughs. He's a fucking *reporter* he ain't a writer. I fell for it myself once too. That guy still has one of my stories and I showed it to him over a year ago HA a*huh* huh…I'da said something to ya but then I thought why the hell should I…

In the open doorway the day is glaring white. Beyond the stone pillar outside in the middle of the entranceway cars whip by on Guerrero. I stare at the whiteness a long time till it burns a haze into my vision and I am blinded to the rest of the bar's brown darkness. All I see is a fuzzy white rectangle. This barking war of the sun this looming this slow eating away of the nerves…

CARVING AT MY FOURTH VAGINA

You're right I am too romantic I knew that centuries ago. Byron I fist fought for his inheritance, kicked me over the head with his club foot the freak; Shelly hell, bottle buddies; Blake I whispered with. But that little scorpion Rimbaud he just balled me up to the size of a pea and popped me down his esophagus like a ripe chunk of hash, washed it down with fire. Bow to that motherfucker as my master in every conceivable way. Yes I'm too romantic I know that so what? So I'll never even be close to rich, or forget that *support* a household even. Like to though, want to with all my soppy heart take care of you but I want to be able to do that on my own terms through a life built upon respect not resignation, through funds made from my talents not compromises. Plunder the circle from outside its rim. The options that are offered are not proper. A B C and D are corrupt. They're *all* wrong. What I want doesn't exist. So now what do I do? And I don't really want to have to take care of you either, I mean other than loving you and all the warmth and strength that that wraps you in, wraps *us* in—but you don't need that anyway you don't need to be taken care of…Most of all I want to be equal partners both of us adding our own certain strengths to the whole. You know, like where I'm lacking in some department you fill the void with your gifts like say I'm terrible with pragmatic concerns like cleaning house or finances but you're good at them so you pick up the slack. And where you have a gap here and there maybe in the more internal adventures I could add my natural attributes and say something like but everyone should be a little sad, makes life more beautiful. You know Nietzsche said the truest laughter comes from those who have truly wept…You see? Balance, back and forth, just like sex. I fill you and you surround me. Symbolism. All the answers are in symbols. I make you whole and you make me whole and together we are one great strength. The main thing is that we find and share the symbols together, work *together*. Is that too romantic for you? I want to live in a forest beside a mountain by a clear swift coldwater stream with rainbows boiling in the shallows to French kiss my fisherman's hook, and that's religion and sport and meditation and happiness and dinner all in one and the seasons will speak to us tell us all we need to know about God and life and that dirty angel called Death. Rivers and fields and forests. Cities are for dead carp.

In the sharp corners of my cocktail napkin I press lines with my thumbnail into the points so that the angle resembles a mons venus. Take great care to shape the lines correctly, proportionate length with a kind of long skinny horseshoe curving around the top of the main straight and more deeply indented line where I dug hard with my nail slid back and forth into the soft paper to get proper articulation. Delicate process to get it just right. Sometimes when I go to draw the curving hood I accidentally obliterate the main line and then have to lift the glass and spin the napkin to a fresh corner. I'm working a third one now when Booster goes hey, buddy. Standing next to me at the rail. Lift my attention from my beautiful little bald porcelainwhite genitalia and he goes you like movies? Movies? Yeah sure… Looks over his shoulder then back at me, holds a video a porn beneath his elbow. Five bucks. Shake my head. It's good man fuckin *hot*. Man I don't even own a tv. Five bucks man it's cheap. I shake him off. How bout a microwave need a microwave? Just picked one up today it's outside. Naw man, no.

Motions with his chin to my blue canvas bag resting on the stool next to me. Carry my notebook and any books I happen to be reading at the time in there. Is he drinkin? Booster asks. No, I say, he's drivin. Designated. Gotta stay straight for the ride home, you know how it is. Got my life in his hands…Wanting the seat he stands waiting for me to remove the bag. C'mon man pick it up. What's that you're makin? Looks like a pussy. Don't use language like that around me man! I say. My girlfriend's picture's in my wallet! I smile at myself that was a good one. I hide the smile from

Booster. C'mon man, he persists, move the bag. I ignore him. If he reaches in here I'll sever the arm neatly at the elbow with my razor sharps. There are plenty other stools. Finally moves off. Creep. Carving at my fourth vagina nursing my fifth drink to death and it just died. Jose! Una mas por favor! I'm careful never to let my tab climb out of control because money's low, way low, and is there nothing for me lord O lordy lord! After a night on tab I stay away for a good week or so to make sure I can pay it off next time I come in. If I don't pay it right away and start buying Joe won't say anything at first, works more subtly than that—chatter disappears, longer to get served, eyes go cold with a kind of numbness. Psychological attack. Deliberately held back once or twice just to watch the shift in his demeanor. His eyes frosted over till finally as I'm about to leave I went well how much do I owe ya Joe? and he said *I wondered when you were gonna pay that goddamn ting!* The clouds lifted then and his eyes thawed. Joe brings the drink over. Gracias Jose. I'm speaking Spanish just to be a stupid fuck. Joe's Irish. He looks at me and I can see the numbers shuffle behind his eyes keeping track. Never writes down a tab, all in his head. Lime suspended in the middle of the glass like that charlatan Koons' basketball in the aquarium. I'd market it as parody to the Modern Museum and get $100,000 if I were a fraud of that guy's caliber. Drink it down instead so it can work its happy magic. There. There's art. And I still have my soul. But is the soul edible? Yes tastes like poison toad brought to frothy boil. I'm still poor. Money's a distraction, makes you mushy makes you always look for the easy way comfort above all else…Comfort drains the eyes. Can't have that and soul too. I'd like to try. Be among the first to succeed where the others bloat and plummet. I'd stay a stiff oily feather and flip'em all off. Can't see why everyone isn't an artist of some kind, or at least an aficionado, and live according- ly. I mean can't understand how they get through without it. Forget the label the word means nothing if the hunt doesn't form infrared lenses over the eyes, sprout fangs to rip open the carcass to see what's inside. The search…Search for what? For what's been taken from us: Paradise. HA! Right. Know better than that… Still, there is something missing, something dreadfully wrong. Where's the magic always suspected? Gotta stay poor to maintain the vision, keep the watch. Tearing and tearing at the carcass and it is not jeweled honey dripping from the hollow belly but crazy mad wasps making a thorny fog. Envious of the others in a way I suppose. I mean my god I'd honestly be so much happier if I wasn't built this way. Sometimes I think I'll just quit, shed all this gloom and struggle and snarling and join the happy dancing crowd and have my piece of smile too. Because really what else is there? I'll knock off the dreamy stuff and stop peeling back the layers and shake this puffy cloud of a head and get a job no not a job a career going in say advertising doing computer animation or something creative like that. Yeah you'd like that wouldn't you Hon? And your mother shit she'd cream all over it…Yeah I could do that and the money the money would just pour right in and I'd get a Jeep Cherokee or Land Cruiser maybe and tool around the hills of the city gleaming and beaming in the sun and I'd finally be living cuz it's just life, right? It's just living. And that's all we're supposed to do anyway, live. You don't see a cat or dog or wolf or squirrel or pigeon (*piggon* is how you used to say it to be cute) or falcon or centipede or deer or cow or trout or chimp or horse or fruit fly or puma or gecko or sea lion or elephant or humming bird or grizzly bear or alligator or any creature killing itself over existence now just relax and enjoy and play the part without having to make sense out of and ask so much from what is obviously meant to be senseless flux and hunger and pain and manipulation and greed and pleasure and death and birth and murder and mystery. I won't take on its weight and be the freak show to this parade any longer, I tell myself. It's not worth it. Simple—forget it…Who needs it? Yeah that's what I'll do, I sometimes tell myself, I'll just be like the rest and dance dance dance…So I start mixing with the other dancers once again and once again I find my feet have taken root and I'm paralyzed and life is not only just to live but to seek the source of growth and awakening and the tremulous shimmering thread stitching through it and my eyes burst with pleading struggle for someone or something to help free my steps but the only thing that will set me free is either an oozy to mow down the entire mob and myself along with them or art, so the choice is art because it is less messy and achieves the same end anyway when done correctly. With art though the murder is more deeply felt because the artist lives with it slowly every day. The murder *is* the art, and once the murder is executed once the metallic blood coats the tongue and the taste swallowed the artist has to keep killing because it is the only thing that satisfies, it is the only thing that makes sense, it is the only thing that brings life where life itself fails. And is there nothing else I feel worthy of my involvement? No nothing...I've looked into the future and saw the demon in my dreams. It's their world they made it they can keep it. The world roasts like a slow pig, and there's too many faces slobbering around the fire to care anymore. I'll sit right here in my own garden mess and watch the finish of the burning with dark glasses on to reflect the flames wiggle. I belong to the secret taciturn land of the dead where eyes are too much like clear fragile glass.

And we all I think suspect there's magic existing out there breathing among us but have never held it in our fingertips. Or rather we all have held it but have failed to recognize it. Or maybe it is that we are so full of magic, actually *born* of it, that we're too close to see. I guess that's what art does, holds up a giant mirror for us to peer into to see the magic briefly. But still it is only a mirror, illusion. Take it away and where does the magic go? Take the mirror away and we are blind once again. On our own then, up to us to find it then—to feel it, to live it. All we can really do is maintain our suspicion and keep the vigil. That's all I'm doing, standing watch. And why always this constant urge to apologize for my life? Darkness forest. World of fire. Original experience. Blue bubble floating from the cracked skull, fleeing spirit, fleeing the field of Time, Shackle King, Body. I dream black whirling birds through the drink of their sky.

MARRIED

Crossing Van Ness at Market Street. The spot. Suddenly see it all again like every time I pass here. Sun just as warm as it was that day. Crossing with you I saw the light change to yellow and suddenly stopped and refused to move another step unless you kissed me. Had hold of your hand and said kiss me here in front of all these people or we're both pancakes, and so you did of course. Meanwhile the light turned red and horns were going and the afternoon yellowbird sun strong and bright and the wind was pushing at us and we're kissing there in the middle of the intersection halting the center lane of traffic on the right side of busy Van Ness Avenue while the other two lanes of cars whipped by either side of us and when our lips finally separated you went not to be outdone *marry* me here in front of all these people. And so not to be topped myself I said I *marry* you and swept my hand theatrically over my heart and we kissed again a quick one and horns were crazy and the sun and wind still strong and busy as we proceeded safely to the curb and so we were married. Remember?

Jesus...

Time makes the long movie of our lives seem to belong to the memory of someone else.

So long ago, now…So long ago...

THE ONE HOLY THING

Girl's long brown hair falls and sways over the back of the bus seat in front of me. My hands rest on my knees. Crooked ends of the hair dangle just above my knuckles straining to tangle in them. My fingers twitch. Gently I clasp the soft ends between two fingers like scissors that refuse to cut, like scissors that has lost its teeth and now can only gum its food, clasp lightly so she will not feel and hold it there cinnamon and soft and smooth as water. It is not like your hair but reminds me of one or two others. In memory of them I see your face rising to the top. Creamy blueflamed greeneyed phoenix. Surprisingly few women in my life that've held me in passion's jaws and made me want to devour them. When I find one I can devour sexually I am hers. Naturally monogamous that way. You love pussy don't you? you asked. Another car episode. I liked doing it in the car, exciting to me, kept it fresh. Twisting around the gear shift to get in between your legs. Like a fishbowl the world coming in through the glass surrounding us. Straight from that hick bar to a dark lane. Never been there before but you knew the spot. How? You love pussy don't you? Watching me from your perch in the driver's seat, watching the pleasure of my feed. Rolled my eyes up into your face staring down at me. Yes. Is it all pussy or just mine? All, but I love yours in particular. Hands hooked under and around your thighs. You grabbed my ears, earlobes, sides of head. Yours only yours I wanted to say but it wouldn't come out. Only moaned a growl into your labia and tasted. I could eat you till all the country milk and meat cows learn to recite the preamble adroitly. Run the girl's hair between my fingers like testing the quality of silk. Passes inspection gloriously. Hold it for a moment longer without moving my fingers. Hold it still and look at it. Thin frozen polished waterfall I want to swim up like a possessed salmon on a suicide sex mission, fertilize till I dry up into a crisp curl on the rocky bank and my eyes are eaten by ravens. Get a swiveling fisheyed view of the bird's viscera as it flaps over treetops. The fish and the raven must be my spirit helpers; they are the two animals for which I feel the most affinity. Fish, and specifically the act of fishing, appear in my dreams with frequent regularity, the most recurring dream theme in my vat of dream pool. And when I see a raven flying overhead I always say to myself there goes my brother. The raven is the most alienated species of the bird kingdom. I am not a beast, I am actually a fishbird. These teeth are just a mask I've strapped on in order to blend in with my environment so I will not get caught and gobbled. Beneath this hard shield of a mask resides a gentle and open terror. And behind that I am a fishbird gone. Fishbird? Piranha and condor…Rub the hair in my fingers again to melt the ice and get the water's current resurging. I WANT TO SWIM IN YOUR HAIR! HEY! WANT MY COCK TO LIVE IN THE SWIM OF YOUR HAIR! DO YOU HEAR ME! HEYYY! The words reverberate against the inner walls of my skull like silver balls rolling around smoothly in there. Of course she doesn't hear. Fingertips have language but it's not auditory. It's *verbal* alright, but the words speak through the electricity of touch, through feeling, and she cannot feel me. Somehow though I sense the words transfer from my finger ends and climb up the strands like telephone wire plugged directly into her brain. She gets my message, I know.

Wait. Now I'm receiving a message.

FUCK OFF ASSHOLE! IT'S ALL I CAN DO TO KEEP FROM TURNING AROUND AND LETTING YOU HAVE IT IN FRONT OF THE WHOLE BUS! NOW DROP THE HAIR! NUT!

I let the ends go free. My hands resume their lonely posts. That's enough. That's all the love I need for now. Have to construct love through stealth these days. Easier that way. That way I still have you but without the distraction of your presence. Or anyone else's. I have love if only in my mind. Know you still love me anyway even though you won't speak to me. Easier for *you* that way. And how could anyone ever replace me?

Doesn't every replaced male say that? Women can fill the gap so easily. That's their edge over men. Men have to wait till the gate opens. Longer wait involved there and much longer line waiting…Alone. I've got to stay alone. Can't give the energy and focus away. A woman demands too much time and effort. Gotta stay hard. Erect. Stay hungry. Coiled meat spring. Deprivation keeps you lean and supple and alive. Light. Fuck I'm a drifting pin feather floating on alligator breath. I've come to the uneasy conclusion that I am capable of loving no one now more than myself. Yet, you are still the only one who could weight me solid. At least while these letters in my mind keep writing themselves. When they stop then I can stop wanting you. When they finish then I know you are finished and I will finally either float away completely or drop like lead and anchor in the bowels of the earth. The coming together of a man and woman, that is magic. The strong elastic pull tugging a man toward a woman and a woman toward a man, that is magic. The speech of a woman's eyes cheekbones nose lips tongue chin neck hair shoulders chest breasts nipples back buttocks fingers belly hips vulva thighs calves toes skin, that is magic. The sweet subtle at long last communication between a man and a woman, the delicate words, soft voice exchange of stories and knowledge, the special language created uniquely between them and only they can speak it, *that* is magic. The man in the woman and the woman surrounding the man, sex, and not even actual physical sex but the *spirit* of sex, *that* is the *only* magic! Sex, the beginning word, the maker and the breaker, the one holy thing on earth. The earth is a colossal cunt/cock locked in perpetual blissful combat, and we are skin packaged products of that combat. Sex is the river that carries us all the way to the big ocean. It is not love that makes the world go round. Love is the semen mortar that holds it all together, the glue that we concoct and dab on. Love comes and goes as we let it. Sex, the spirit of sex, is the push that keeps the whole thing spinning. It's the spirit of sex that takes us all in. It is the underlying structure of all things, the still spot of our radius. It's our creator, the air about us engulfing us surrounding us invisibly in the warmth of its leaden lighted sphere; it's the origin of our consciousness, the motivational activeity, the shaping of our lives the ruin of our brains the stretch of our happiness; it's what takes us all in and folds the final shore to the stars of our night—the Shiva dance insinuating barefooted in the shaky forming milk of our bones and over the shard bones catacombing articulation in the bloated space of the grave.

All this time clawing life apart and only in pasting the pieces back together do I see what was already there before me. And I hear you now cursing me with laughter.

At the next stop a young woman in tight jeans boards the bus out of the strong pallid light biting through the white sheet sky enveloping the streets in a giant squint. She takes a few seconds to pause at the entrance after feeding her money into the till seemingly to allow her eyes to adjust to the slight dimness of the bus before moving further inside. When she's recovered enough and begins to walk down the aisle the bus lurches and she's thrown running forward a few steps. She grips the overhead rail bracing against the centrifugal force, stopping briefly next to me till it eases off. Her hip leans against my shoulder. Camel toes of her crotch are at eyelevel. I lean my face slightly forward to my left and inhale deeply but there is no scent. Inhale again, still nothing. And then the bus steadies and she moves toward the rear.

FELLINI IS A CARROUSEL

All these false boundaries the world constructs that we think are so sound, so powerful, all these different countries cities abstract politics we construct for ourselves, staking out landmasses, coasts, everything inside this line is ours, stay on your own side or watch out *trouble*...All these walls and buildings and technologies and weapons we erect and create to separate and dominate and protect ourselves from one another, to show our intelligence and abilities off, to advance the speed of business, get the edge, reap reward—sell consume produce build erect sell consume produce build erect... The endless cycle...And look what we've done aren't we great? Yes, but still not quite...It's all too thin and tenuous to really believe in. One great heave and sigh and shrug of the earth, one great expulsion of breath and loosening of its belt and it'll all come down around us and then we'll all just be humans again together, one huge consciousness group with hoes in one hand and phallus spears of fire in the other guarding and tending the planet. We keep missing the point over and over...I love wandering at night the city takes on such a different face. Purer mask of quiet. God what time is it anyway, after 2? Quiet neighborhood streets. There really is beautiful architecture here. All these bay windows and redwood Victorians with such minute arabesque detail curlicuing and spirally. No place like it, style all its own. All go into the ocean one day in crumple shards so let's enjoy it now. Gonna have to walk all the way back home, too late for a bus they've stopped running to my side of town by now. So clear tonight... Plenty of stars, dappled silver placenta, but no moon. If you climb to a hill view and look out over the lights of the city thrown out like a web of lightseeds scattered and then look up at the web of stars overhead you'll see the connection. Crossing into the Panhandle from Fell Street at Clayton; smell of eucalyptus emanating from trees. Little strip of forest wedged between two busy one ways like a runway for pterodactyls. Ancient forest feel to these trees. They're enormous bluegreen veiny butterflies standing on hind legs with their toes planted shallowly in the ground.

Shadows...Shadows and trees and still eucalyptus permeation. Two small silhouettes approaching ahead on the pathway. A dog and...is that a little kid? What's a little kid doing walking a dog at 2 AM? Long chain. Closer. White dog. Pit bull. Watch it buddy I'll bite back, you just be cool. That's not a kid. A woman. Dwarf. Dog comes first pulling her behind on the end of the chain. Who's walking who here? Dog looks at me and I stop so he won't get spooked. Black rubber sponge nose stuck to the toe of my shoe sniff sniff. Shade, the woman says to the dog. Follow the long chain with my eyes to the little voice attached to the end. Shade come on, she says bringing her end of the chain to a slackened rest at the rear of the standing dog. It's alright, I say, and drop my hand for the dog to smell then stroke his ears. He's white and you call him Shade? Yeah, she says. Actually it's Lampshade. Ever see those dogs right from the vet's office wearing those white plastic funnels around their heads? Look like lampshades? Well *I* think they look like lampshades anyway. S'pose I could've named him Funnel, but that's not as fun. Those dogs are just so funny lookin they just make me laugh. Remind me of a circus and I love circuses, the clowns...I love to laugh. So when I got him—he's kinda intimidating and I like that for protection, but I didn't wanna live with that all the time ya know, like living with a bully—I named him Lamp-shade as a joke really, to soften him down. I don't know, I got a weird sense a humor.

That *is* funny, I say, and stroke down the side of the dog saying Lampshade softly. He is one solid mass of muscle bulge seething strength.

I don't sleep very well, she says, so sometimes I get up in the middle of the night and take him for a walk. He likes it.

Kneeling beside her on the pathway I am just barely smaller than her. Normal-size head, that is, the size of an average woman's, but her limbs are tiny bulbous reductions like knotted balloons. Surprisingly pleasant voice. Why is that a surprise?

Yeah, I'm a night prowler too, I say. Just something about the night, ya know? Something goes off inside me and I just gotta get out. I have dark rhythms I think. The night seems both safe and dangerous at the same time. I like that. I'm a little weird too, I guess.

I like foggy nights best, she says. They're more like a dream, or an old black and white movie. You know, Humphrey Bogart…Makes me feel like I'm sleepwalkin. Maybe I am…Makes me feel like I'm not losin any sleep anyway. On clear nights like tonight I always feel like Jesus you stupid you should be in bed you have to work in the mornin, and then I usually wake up tired the next day. After foggy nights I don't wake up tired at all.

I stand up and I am a giant. I am a eucalyptus. I look at the trees watching over us flut-fluttering softly their wings in the darkness, wondering if they'd adopt me. I smile. But then I look back down at her and I feel self-conscious so kneel again and grab the dog, shake the furskin of his neck which is a taught cylinder of steel. He's a good dog, I say. Yeah she says. His collar jangles as I play with him. He sneezes and shakes his head and unrolls his tongue like a carpet. Why do dogs have black tar lips? I stand again and prepare to go my way, and miles to go before I…and she smiles up into my face and tilts her head slightly, like there's more she wants to say but it's not coming. She stands there looking up at me that way smiling and I feel funny looking down at her so lower my eyes and take a step forward saying well have a good—Can I ask you something? she interrupts and moves in front of me. Shit she's gonna ask for money didn't look like a panhandler never can tell. Uh-huh sure, I say. Can I…she says. Can I give you a blowjob? She looks right into my face and I am a giant and she is half of me poured into a shot glass. Suddenly I want a drink. I don't want anything, she says, I just want…Comes closer. I don't get many men, she says, I just want to feel it. I mean you can have more if you want but I'm too embarrassed to ask for that. She touches my hip with her small hand and her eyes are laid so gently up into my face. I do get hard. That *is* a surprise. I let her back me pushing at my hip against the smooth huge trunk of a eucalyptus. The bark is half peeled in long twisted striations like Christmas ribbon spiraling over the edge of a package. The chain of the dog is wrapped in her left fist. Standing in the shadow against the tree she stands before me and takes it in her mouth without the slightest bend of her body. I watch it go in and out of her normal-size head. Turns her normal-size eyes up to me, checking to see how she's doing by the gauge of my face. I don't know what it tells her, but I read gratitude in hers. She turns her eyes back down. I look around. No one. It's late. It's quiet. Nothing but eucalyptus trees stretching batting tender wings and smells and shadows and grass and dark blue sky and stars and me and a dwarf and a pit bull. A few cars go by on Fell but we're in the shadows so they don't see. It's the experience that matters. Oh you wouldn't understand...I have to do things for art, to write. Leaving you was one thing, one *big* thing, and this is just one more...Just as sex with you was the passion and the passion was the love so tightly entangled they couldn't be separated, so now the love is the memory and the memory the passion. Made you come 20 times in a row once. I counted. The record. At least you let me believe it was the record. Can't imagine anybody taking you further than that, though. Your knees had no strength left in them. I had to help you to the bathroom. You couldn't speak, only in stutters. Only in breathy stutters. But I counted and it was 20 times from start to finish. Toward the end they were coming every ten seconds and your body seemed out of control, in shock. I stopped at 20 because I was afraid I was going to kill you. GIRL DIES OF EXCESSIVE ORGASMS. I could see the headline...Scared me... Impossible but I want to write every memory down as it comes, to dispel you and be rid of you. This is an exorcism. I look down at the tiny body attached to my cock. Fellini is a carrousel in my mind. We are all freaks, just more obvious in some. Some people embody the word physically, but we all share the same circus tent. There are strange things dwelling within us all like dark creatures we keep on leashes out of sight from one another. When I see a deformed man on the street I want to embrace him because he expresses exactly how I feel inside. And I'm trivializing nothing. He is my comrade and my hero. What's worse, freak inside or out? It glides between her lips in and out glistening in flashes. I put my hands on her shoulders. Taught and round. My fingers fall down and cover her shoulder blades like folded cupid wings. The dog still on the end of the chain held tightly in her fist is sniffing a spot of grass… I don't watch anymore, feel the hard wood of the trunk running along my spine and look up the branches of the tree shooting like a ladder into the sky. The stars are there…I say that quietly to myself. The stars are still there…I stand staring up at the sky. And wait.

THE RUSSIAN

Ghosts and dreams
In dawn's mercury
Circle about the
Velvet chamber
Sniffing sharply
Snarling at one another
In accusations of sadness

I put the pen down and push the napkin forward on the bar and wait for Tony to finish tending to the couple at the far corner so he can come down here and collect my poem so I can collect my pint. That's a pretty good exchange—poems for pints. If only the rest of syphilization operated on this principle I'd be a sassy well-fed wealth of a gentle giant presume. This is my best one tonight I think. The next one will be about your eyebrows, ode to your eyebrows, sharp and thick so distinctive just like your nose very unique—and your eyes …your eyes…Tony takes the napkin, reads it silently, smiles nods and puts it in his pants pocket with the other two poems I wrote earlier as barter. Then as he

sets my pint of Anchor Steam cool amber and tan headed in front of me he says I like that one the most so far,
gimme another one. Let's see how many you can do in
one night, man. And I say shit you better tap another
keg.

Tony moves back to the other end of the bar laughing, pushing his hat to the back of his head.

What punky bravado you take on when you drink
boy, I tell myself. You're lucky if you can drag another
line out of your soggy brain yet alone an entire poem.
Eyebrows...No forget the eyebrows, that's not Tony's
speed. Probably renege on the beer if I hand him
something like that, the prick.

Take another napkin from the stack twisted like a
white cyclone in front of me at the inner lip of the bar.
It's already smooth but I run my hand over it anyway as
if to straighten it out, just to feel it. I sit looking at it.
White white white...I drink down half my pint staring
down at the little square of pure winter before me. Then
drink some more...This is stupid you've got stacks of
poems you can rely on just put one of *those* down.
That'd be cheating. The point to this little game remember Blu I tell myself is to try and come up with something new each time. It's an exercise, see? And you're
gonna stick to the rules you've set yourself for this
exercise. Even though Tony wouldn't know the difference *you'd* know so stick to it or...Or what? Or well
what nothing I guess just do it...

Singing singing singing in my head head, song, song,

little song pieces tearing up and flying, songs flying, fly off, off and out, gone…I pick up the pen.

Songs in pieces
Torn and winged
We die

A soft warm hand suddenly caresses the back of my neck. I jump in my seat. Bluuu, how are you?

Uh hi Fa…uh…Fab—…I'm sorry how do you say your name again?

Fabrianasha, but just call me Fab. I don't mind.

No I told you I won't call you that. Si'down Fabria—…uh…do you mind if I just call you Fabria, it's easier for me.

No, of course not, Bluu.

There's that smile again, pretty teeth, she's letting them out to say hello too. Hello there pretty little Russian teeth…She sits on the stool to my right.

What's that? she says, meaning the napkin.

Oh nothing, I say turning it over.

You were writing, I disturbed you.

I should know better than doin that in a bar anyway, I say. I swallow the last of my beer and wave at Tony. He comes over and picks up the new napkin. It's not finished but I let him look. He flips it around to where the writing is then makes a crinkled face. It's *OK*, he says, but you're slippin early Blu. Yeah yeah just give Fabria a drink you shit, I tell him.

She orders vodka straight and pays for it herself.

I'm sorry I'm out of money tonight or I'da bought that for you.

I don't want you to buy me a drink, the Russian says.

Oh…

Tony brings another pint. He's got a smoke dangling from his lips and I ask for one. Digs two fat fingers into his breast pocket and drops a Marlboro on the bar and goes away smiling at the Russian under his hat brim. She smiles back and they lock eyes until he's gone to the far end of the bar. Then she lowers her head tucking the smile into her chest. I put the cigarette between my lips and pat myself looking for a light. So what are you doing tonight Fabria? I mumble, cigarette wagging like a sprung diving board.

Hmm? She lifts her head and turns to me. I'm still patting myself.

Shit I thought I had a light…I said what are you doing?

Oh, I'm just out of work. It was very slow toniight. Here…Fabria hands me a book of matches that says RED ROOM in gold letters across the red cover. I open it and am met with bright red-tipped matches shouldered together in tight soldier rows your toes the exact color you painted your toenails I used to make fun because you'd always paint them the same color always the same flaming red nail polish over and over you'd hold your feet up in the air with your hands at your ankles when we made love I'd look over my shoulder at them up there I liked it.

What? the Russian goes.

What what? I say.

You're smiling, she says.

Am I? Take a picture that doesn't happen too often.

Bluuu you are crazy.

Smiling down at the matches I break one of the toes and light my smoke. Hand them back. Red Room, huh? That where you work? A cloud gropes twisting into the air.

Yes but I'm quitting. The woman I work for all she does is yell at me. I am a dancer not a waitress I tell her that, even though I don't dance anymore. I quit to stay here and I can't get a San Francisco troop to hire me. There are many dancers here and they are very good.

Forgive me for asking this but could it have anything to do with your breasts? They're umm…pretty large for a ballet dancer, aren't they?

No, she smiles, they have never gotten in my way.

Her smile is so lush so seductive I can feel myself going to her, my will rising toward her, toward her lips, her teeth, her black twinkling eyes, and I am going to have this woman tonight and I am going to have this woman tonight…

The only thing that gets in my way is making money. I have to worry about that instead of dancing. This woman I work for she only hired me because she's from Moscow too. I told her I was a very respected bal-lerina in Moscow and she said in America you are a very horrid waitress. She is a pig and I hate her. I'm quitting. Toniight maybe is my last niight, or maybe next week.

She takes a sip from her drink, pausing only long enough to swallow.

Oh I don't really hate her but she yells too much. And I don't have any money or hardly any clothes. I had to leave all my bags when I left my troop. The only things I had were what I was wearing when I left. I had to sneak away out of the hotel where we were staying or they wouldn't have let me go. I borrowed these clothes for work from the woman I'm staying with.

The Russian's wearing a white short sleeve shirt and short black skirt. And no stockings. Typical waitress uniform except the no stockings part. She's got hairy arms I notice, lots of long brown hairs crosshatching the white flesh of her forearms. Never saw those hairs last time, course I *was* distracted...I want to munch on those hairs with horselips...

She and her husband, Fabria says, they are so niice. They are Indian. They let me stay for nothing. I have only to clean the apartment and cook a meal each day and they let me stay. They even introduced me to the woman I work for.

Were they the friends you were waiting for the night we met?

What? Oh yes—Ananda and Prahni. They are so niice. But I want to leave. I'm beginning to feel not so comfortable. Ananda thinks I am bothering her husband. I can't help it if Prahni looks at me. I don't do anything. My robe just falls open sometimes, then I look up and Prahni's smiling so I smile back. I don't want to seem…what's the word?...

Ungrateful?

Yes un*grate*ful they've done so much for me so I smile and let him look. Ananda doesn't like—

Fabria I want you to stay with me tonight.

What?

I'm not looking at her I'm staring into my beer, but peripherally I see that she's allowing her eyes to eat into my profile. Instantly I feel her offense and regret my clumsy ineptitude but I can't stop now, I have to find out…*And you don't owe me anything*…Her words from the first night have never left me, and I want her desperately tonight. The emptiness is unbearable…And who are you with tonight and who are you with?

What did you say? she asks again.

I turn to her this time. I said *I*—want *you*—to stay with *me* tonight.

Hey you guys in love? Booster's stubbly face pops between us, his long bushy ponytail swishing from side to side as he flips his head from me to the Russian then back to me. His eyes direct ours down to a set of hand-cuffs cradled furtively in his hand. I got another pair too, he says, both ov'em five bucks. He stares directly into my face.

Get the *fuck* outta here!

OK just tryin ta help ya know, I mean just tryin ta

help he says as he moves further down the bar wriggling his shoulders and shrugging his palms in the air like a monkey. As I watch him eye another couple from his new position I see Fabria walk past and into the ladies room. Good time for me to go too, I guess. And as I swing open the door Bugs' scraggly gray head pokes out wide-eyed and low from behind the partition. No door on the stall. Rocket's standing in the middle of the room holding something under the long hook of his nose, sniffing. Give Blu a hitta that shit, Bugs says, and when Rocket gets done he dips into the Winston cigarette package held upright in his left hand with what I now see to be a house key in his right and brings out a tiny white hill balanced on the end. Well c'mon *hurry-up!* Rocket says, standing there holding the key out to me. I walk over do it and step to the urinal all in one fluid motion. Behind me I hear the door squeal open and then closed and I know Rocket's gone and *Jee*sus this pisser smells like a *zoo*! I pull the neck of my tshirt over my grimace and nose to filter the stink and leave it there like a bandit as I piss. You loved zoos. Every new city we went to you had to see the zoo. Find them terribly sad places myself but you just loved to watch the animals. The sadness eluded you somehow and I could not show you. More than that, was unwilling to try—unwilling to shatter your pleasure and wonder over the natural beauty. Giraffes were your favorite…I must admit though I did enjoy the New Orleans zoo. Lucky enough to get to the alligator compound at feeding time.

Whole butchered chickens stuck on the end of long poles stretched out and held under their noses. Took a few seconds for them to see it but then SNAP in the bat of an eye the terrible mouth crushed the yellow-white little body into disappearance and the sound was a terrifying thunder I went around imitating the whole rest of the hot afternoon (Bright idea I had going to New Orleans in August, wasn't it? Steaming hot jungle…) by slapping my palms together in a sudden cupped clap PLAP. And when the jaws missed the first time it was PLAP PLAP double terror.

Hey theah man, Bugs calls from inside the stall. Jesus this is embarrassin takin a dump like this. No privacy. Like a dog takin a shit on the sidewalk.

I know, I laugh through my shirt, that incredibly vulnerable look they get.

Nutt'n you can do about it, ya gotta go ya gotta go. Hell done it in worse places. Done it on the back of a Greyhound bus once, waitin for the crappah. Some fuckah in theah and I couldn't hold it. Did it right theah in the middle of the aisle.

Walk out to Bugs' laughter reverberating against the walls of the restroom as my shirt slides down off my face. I begin to taste the kerosene impurity drip at the back of my throat. I want to spit but swallow hard instead. Back at my spot at the bar I wash back the taste with beer. The Russian's seat is still empty. Sniffing and rubbing my nose with the back of my hand my eyes drift absently toward the ladies room. Walked right by her and didn't see.

Sitting at the far end of the bar the Russian's smiling as Tony stands next to her hunching over on his elbows inside the break of the bar where it flips up to let the bartender in or out. They're looking into each other's eyes.

I place another napkin in front of me. The kerosene taste is still strong in my mouth. Coke is for dolts but if you place another little white hill in front of me I'd climb it again. The desire to intensify our lives overrides all rational judgment even to the point where the body decays in its tracks. We kill ourselves to live more, *feel* more. So what if we eat ourselves away in the process. Time's big teeth are eating away at us anyway. Time has the biggest teeth of all and they're gonna get us no matter what no outrunning them so we might as well use them to our advantage. We've always lived our lives with a clear and everpresent knowledge of our own deaths, and so have been made wise to what is proper in this life, and conduct ourselves accordingly. We are ready for death because we've run beside it all along, it is our companion and cannot take us by surprise now. Not many others who can say that. We've learned to use death—why do I keep saying *we*?—as a tool to live. As I pick up the pen Tony's laugh sails through the room. Good thing we're not friends, alliances can be restricting.

On the napkin I write swiftly:

Swift robed
The crooked princess
Dwarf streaming
Red streamers in her hair
Kiosk lips
Limp night air, presume
Hungry risk
Stare the stars into a fevered guide

This one's coming with me, I'm even impressing myself now.

As I put the napkin in my pocket I'm reminded of those matches and your toes.

Every little every little *the* littlest THING reminds me of you. Jesus *Christ* matches are conjuring your *toes* for fucksake! When will it end! I expect to see your face at every corner. The other day I almost ran hysterical into the Backyard Laundromat on 17th and Church because I saw you or *thought* I did folding clothes in the window as I passed from the other side of Church Street. She wore a green cardigan like you used to wear and had honey-colored hair just like you tied back just like you used to wear it. I only saw her from behind but that was all I needed it was you and I couldn't believe you'd actually come back and live in San Francisco without telling me. Cars kept passing and then there was a train and then more cars and as I waited to cross the street staring at the girl in the window at *you* in the window my eyes glued to the back of your head the traffic nothing but smeared color and bright flashes between us not believing it was you and yet it couldn't be anyone else, staring as the cars passed she finally turned around and *oh* my foolish desperate stupidity and oh Jesus what the hell am I doing without you here at the edge of the earth where water laps all around me like a bear's tongue and the sea and sky eat each other in a horizon smile, and why can't I just forget you already...

You'd wear that green cardigan while making pizza for us in our old apartment that winter, brushed the wisps of hair out of your face with the back of your wrist as you worked because your hands were all foody, and you wouldn't let me help—I kept eating the ingredients piled waiting on plates in little brown sausage blob piles and green pepper piles and big mozzarella mound, waiting on their plates while you worked the dough...I *did* keep eating the stuff but that wasn't entirely why you wouldn't let me help, though you'd yell at me for picking. Mostly it was just your kitchen your space and you didn't want to share your territory. Shit you shoulda pissed around the perimeter of the linoleum. Our first Christmas Eve together you cooked a honey-glazed chicken with wild rice and broccoli and no girlfriend had ever made me dinner like that before. I probably didn't let it show enough but I was impressed as hell, and I didn't quite love you then but that was the first big opening of my heart for you. Nice tight black dress and black stockings I peeled off you on the living room floor after the meal. Sex and food are mixed up together like a crazy eternal yin yang. How long's it been? Nearly a year since we've seen each other, six months since we've spoken. And the letters sent to you in between unanswered...I had a dream last night. Let me tell you about it. Took place at my parents' house. No one there just us. You came over out of the blue unannounced, came walking through the door and we stood for a moment looking at each other, not saying anything. Your eyes showed embarrassed pain and had to keep looking down away as if self-conscious of giving too much over to me. But then you became bold and your gaze stiffened with cool resolve and would not leave my face, and your big eyes were firm but sensitive too, tender, even sympathetic, a smile dancing somewhere behind them like a butterfly about to land on a flower but never does, fluttering endlessly around it. And I was so happy to see you but couldn't smile either; the pain of knowing we were over was too great for me. I couldn't get past it. Slowly then we gently embraced. And then we were naked and lying on the living room carpet, that ugly orange shag carpet that my parents had in their home for 25 years and were oblivious to its offense, lying on our sides facing each other, touching, looking into one another's eyes but still saying nothing. Suddenly then we're still lying that way but the scene transposed to my father's bed and there you finally broke the silence, saying that you love me, that you'll always love me and you just wanted to tell me that. You came just to tell me that. And we were naked and touching, almost making love but not; we never made love completely in the dream, just always *almost*. And I woke with a happy sadness, feeling like you had finally after months broken your silence and we had finally communicated and there was some semblance of resolution between us now. And immediately, while lying there still in the leaden predawn light reflecting in the glow of where I'd just been, reflecting on what I'd just seen and felt, fresh from secret travel to another velvety realm, fresh from your arms and the lushness of that, immediately I was overcome with the strangest feeling. I felt sure that you had just experienced a similar kind of dream. Somehow I had the deepest sensation that we had just spoken to each other and although I have no way of validating this feeling I believe it, I am convinced and committed to it with all my being. It happened, we spoke telepathically, spiritually to one another through dreams and that's all I can say because I know it, although I can't say how I know I just do. Sometimes all we have is our instinct and intuition to fall back on, and our faith in the guiding light of those powers. In a letter I wrote you once, one you actually responded to, I said: *the rhythm of our spirits will always dance together*. I meant it. I know you probably only took it as just another pretty line, but it came from an unintelligible knowledge somewhere deep within the psyche. I didn't even know fully *myself* then, at the time I wrote it, from what depth and wealth that line had sprung; I only knew that it was true in the innermost reaches of myself...No, I meant it, and this dream proved it, at least to me. We met and swam circling veils around each other like fishtails in the land of dream. And our love lived, *lives*…

Ancient songs
She sang
Her eyes asked
What is your life?

A feeling of being
Overwhelmed, aware,
And not quite sure
Of anything…except
Things are not
As they should be

This new napkin is suddenly ripped out from under my hands like paper ripped out of a typewriter and replaced immediately with a pint. Get your girlfriend outta here will ya Blu, Tony says. She keeps try'nda stick'er hand down my pants. I'm *workin* fer chrissake!

Ain't *my* girlfriend. And gimme that poem back!

Doesn't hear me, he's already on his way over to the opposite side of the bar away from the Russian, tucking the napkin in his jeans without even looking at it this time. Goddammit I wanted that one too. What was it now?…

Ancient songs
She sang
Her eyes

…uh eyes…eyes…her eyes…*asked!*—Oh Bluu you got another drink, I was going to buy you one. Fabria sits back down beside me.

I don't want you to buy me a drink, I say. I don't even want *this* one. I pick up the beer and gulp half of it and set the glass back down. Grabbing the napkin and pen together in my fist I jam them in my jacket pocket. I'm gonna go, seeya around, I say and get off the stool.

Aren't I going with you?

Listen you didn't seem too excited about the idea before so let's—

I didn't like the way you asked. You made me sound like a…I don't know, I didn't like it.

Alright well I'm leaving now it's up to you if you wanna come or not, I say and start heading for the door. I look back over my shoulder only once as I go, for about a half second, and see the Russian throwing back her drink. I wait for her just outside the entrance beneath the big upside down parachute of the neon glass twinkling twinkling gold.

MIDNIGHT MIDLIFE

Fog is cutting through the indigo of the night sky where a few white flecks of stars peer down from the heavens' leathery murk. Inland from the ocean the fog drifts its thick damp wool over the western districts, but when it hits Twin Peaks at the heart of the city that wool splits open and spills down over the rim of the hills, slowly moving forward and bowing apart at the same time like thin gray arms outspread trying to hug my neighborhood in a gigantic lovesoul floating vellum island embrace...From the roof of my apartment building the Russian and I sit in the cool steady wind on the tiny-round-pebbled surface and watch the fog's long gray spindle arms grow longer above us through the sky. We are sitting crosslegged pretzel style facing each other knees to knees, the quart bottle of Budweiser to my right. The beer was a little gift Fabria purchased for me on the walk over from the 500. She's not having any herself though, doesn't like beer. Fine with me. Through the thin screen of darkness I see Fabria looking at me. Externally her eyes are like a cat's, football shaped and slanting upward at the outer corners. But they are also piercing and wise too like a cat's, vaguely inquisitive, curious, both knowing and wanting to know. Her eyes give the feeling of cautious invitation and luxuriousness, make me want to both drape them almost scornfully around me like warm black velvet, scornfully because of their opulence, and shield myself from them in a blush. Your eyes always made me want to just dive right in like plush green pools fringed with tall black vegetation (always wore the mascara a bit heavy on your thick long lashes, made them pop to such seductive comehitherish proportion that I could never resist when they turned to me).

The wind blows at the Russian's back making her hair flutter and whip around the sides of her face in stringy whirls. She seems beautifully witchlike. She's looking at me unblinking, unsmiling, as if waiting for the solution to a mystery to illuminate itself into existence. I grab the bottle and raise the small glass mouth to mine and tip back my head and the beer flows in imitation of a water cooler. Tip it back down then repeat the performance once again and return the bottle to its bed of pebbles. For lack of conversation and the uneasiness created by it my impulse is to say thanks for the beer just to get things going, but I've already said it earlier and don't feel up to servility however minor just to hear myself say something (words are too precious to merely fill the air with like dull empty bubbles) so I don't say anything and look back at her. She gathers the unruly ribbons of hair in her right fist and twists them together, holding them briefly over her right shoulder across her collarbone, but when she releases them they untangle instantly and fly again. She hasn't shifted her eyes from me in the least and I am intrigued by this girl but what do I say? I can't think of a damn thing to say and why does she keep looking at me like that like she's trying to fit the pieces of my puzzle together it's *my* puzzle dammit I like the pieces askew and messy and missing get your fucking eyes *off* me!...I stand up abruptly, turn, take five quick sprinting steps toward the front of the building then tuck my feet up under me in the air, in the helix of my giant leap, jumping as far as I can forcing my head forward to gain more momentum, but at the very end as gravity exudes its power over my body I contract myself a bit controlling the full thrust of possible distance and skid pebbles a perfect two point landing six inches from the edge. I stand looking down three stories out over 18th Street now, my back to the Russian. The 33 bus crawls by below and my head turns with its passing. There's a big 3303 running down the top of it painted in black block numerals through the center of the white roof. I watch the wheels at the end of the two power poles trailing behind the bus as they slide along the electric wires stretched above the street, the source of the bus's mobility, and I wonder how many volts it takes to move that thing and how crispy would I be fried if I flop my body across those wires down there?

Midnight midlife youth, I say, not exactly shouting it but still it comes out pretty loud. The age of magic, black summit. Wishing at death through the minion of innocent play.

I stand there and smile.

That didn't impress me you know! the Russian yells to me.

I twist my head back at her without disturbing my planted stance.

I don't care what it did or didn't do for you, I say, *that* was for me. Most things I do are usually for me, or so I've been told anyway.

Still standing there at the edge of the building I turn around now to face her. The wind is strong and it pours into my face and I feel myself teeter a little in its force. My jacket is unzipped and the wind throws it open at my hips like familiar legs straddling me. Down the long flat of the roof to the next building which, because built on the slope of a hill, towers over the roof I stand on, I see in the orange Halloween light of a window the black shadow of a figure. It stands there with something in its hand it's drinking from as it looks out toward us into the night. It's dark up here I'm sure whoever it is can't see us and even if they can what's to see? I turn back around to the edge and look out. Wind rushes into my ear shells turning everything else silent; the whole world the wind just turns it off. Straining leg muscles taught in flight, the tshh sound of the pebbles as my feet nail their arrival, and the edge so close, so close…My whole wonderful leap flashes through my mind, then flashes again …So goddamn close…I smile as I absorb the rooftops and dotted lights and darkness stretching out before me, feeling triumphant for no particular reason at all but triumphant nonetheless, as if I'm on a huge stage and the city is my adoring audience watching every move I make. But then, suddenly, as always, as if a whisper, a shadow of a whisper even, the lightest and most undetectable of touches brushes across my mindscape and my smile fades in its presence ephemeral. For a split second it touches me but that's all it needs, that thing whatever it is that hovers so diligently at my shoulder and watches has observed my leap too and I feel it enclosing me in a frown shaking its head in a psychic tsk tsk making me conscious of ostentatiousness, and then it is gone. My ghostly other that keeps me in line, leaves its message like a tap on the noggin then slips right back into its invisible pocket, back to its watchful post and waits with knuckles to its chin. And although I really did make that jump just for me there is a part of me too that is very glad the Russian was here to witness it, to feel my intensity, I imagine. I think of the times, say, while walking down the street seeing people climb into their BMW or Mercedes or Lexus and I've looked at them with an abject face formulating words like *ostenta-tiousness is the seal to the coffin*, and here I am showing off for this girl on a dark rooftop. Humble in the hands of the gambol of the gods, remember Blu?

That's how you were gonna live, that's the philosophy you set for yourself. But my ostentatiousness is different from theirs. Mine comes from self-expression, theirs from flashing their money—and what's that? Where's the self in that, the personal gratification in that bloated display? What have they actually achieved within themselves? Ahh I think way to goddamn fucking much it's just life it's just life it's *just* LIFE!...Can't seem to convince myself of this somehow. It's how you live that makes all the difference...to how clearly you see...

I lied to you before, I tell Fabria as I walk back to her and sit down.

What? You lied? What was it you lied about?

I've never read any Thomas Mann.

Oh Bluu...she laughs.

But I do love Hermann Hesse. I wasn't lying about that. He's one of my favorites.

What did you jump like that for Blu?

Nothing. Forget it, I say. I don't know, there are some things you don't talk about. There are some things you say only to yourself. Sometimes though, ya know, in certain situations, action can feed the brain. I dunno, let's drop it.

It scared me a little bit though, she says, and smiles.

I look at her and see excitement sparking in her eyes. So she liked it after all hmm? Got her juices trickling? Beauty and fear, the two forces that penetrate the human psyche most deeply. Couple them together into the same alchemistic storm and they can be transcendental, spiritually heightening. I aspire to inspire that storm. I want to be those two forces the white of beauty and the black of fear intertwined like serpents, a new caduceus. Why am I telling you this? Just another little fishy swimming across my brain pan why shouldn't you see it? I want to tell you everything, explain myself to you totally, though I know you won't get it or even care.

I look over and the shadow is still standing at its window.

Let's uh…go down, I say.

Yes my legs are cold, Fabria says, and I look and she's got chicken skin and I grab the big awkward brown bottle half full and we climb the narrow iron ladder down the face of the building and the bottle klinks against the side of the ladder as I descend and when we reach the next landing climb through my darkened bedroom window and into my bed and the emptiness I sought to fill with the Russian still remains, only now it's cloaked behind the red cloth of our passion. We're just two skeletons with meat attached pushing desperately at each other in the dark; two frames of bones digging at each other like a child's hand digs to the bottom of a cereal box for the prize lodged there that is as much chintzy and hollow as it is fleeting and glorious. And this is what I call Skeletal Vision, my plague and malady…eyes that burn all the way to the bone, burn the veils away layer by layer like an apocalyptic heat and see all the way to the end, to the emptiness of the core where only charred sticks lay propped against each other alone and lonely in smoldering wind—eyes so heavy with sight they weigh me to one spot and all I can do is sit and look at a vacant world and rot because with eyes like these how can you act or do anything except simply exist, function outwardly while internally disintegrating...How can you participate when all that's offered all you see before you is a sham a hopeless dirty sham cheating the very soul right out of our lives?

When you reach this stage, when you possess this kind of vision there's nowhere to go but down down done. You're at the floor of the River Abyss and they might as well float the funeral wreath—you're done... Unless...And this is what I realize while making love with Fabria, hearing her laughter at the onslaught and fit of each orgasm...Unless you learn to laugh at the monster!

Learn to *laugh* at the *monster!* Laugh at the world and it can never take anything away from you as long as you know *why* you're laughing—as long as you retain within yourself the black memory abyss of the vision that has been granted to you like a used thorny crown. If you stare into the black long enough the colors will come. And I say *you* but mean *me*, and I feel this girl soft beneath me all sighs and laughter and she's just taught me the meaning of life without even knowing. And the act we've so heatedly plunged ourselves into and steeped ourselves in *is* the world and *is* holy, but the paradox is that it means absolutely nothing at the same time. Its holiness resides precisely in balance with its hollowness.

And I feel it now, I feel at this moment the swirl of every darkness leaving me like bats flapping; all the dirt and corrosion is being washed from my gullet and nothing can touch me now because nothing is all it all is. Even you are leaving me, leaving me as you are burrowing deeper within me melding with my being where you will stay forever, because once I love I love for all of Time. I feel you melting into my center where you cannot torment me any longer only move along with the cotton candy procession of years eventually back with me into the watery blur dream void beginning, back to where it all began, where we will hold hands again, where every being holds hands finally and become one. I feel it now, the struggle to end the film life after life with a smile, and the desire for that smile.

JOE

If you wanna drink Blu make it yourself I ain't makin the fuckin ting, Joe mutters as he walks out from behind the bar around the corner carrying the register trays into the backroom. 2 AM—shift over, door bolted, now all Joe has to do is count the night's earnings in the back and put it in the safe, and I have free full reign of the bar. It's like this about every night depending upon the bartender's mood. Every night at closing the crowd is swept out except for a few select regulars who just sit hunched over their drinks and try to make themselves look as small and invisible as they can while the rest are pushed out the door. Makes you feel special in a way to know that when a bartender shouts EVERYONE OUT LET'S GO! he's not talking about you. There's something warm in that.

Just so happens tonight I'm the only regular left, and I think Joe's relieved. I know I am. I don't think Joe's much in the mood for dealing with many people tonight. I know I'm not. One person he could handle though—yeah that's OK I think. One person's alright with me too, seeing how we're separated by an entire room at the moment anyway. Yeah, I think one person's OK for both of us.

While Joe's in the back I swing behind the bar onto the slatted flooring and start fixing myself another gin and tonic. Feels strange on this side. Look at all these bottles, all the pretty color and shine...There's too much power behind here that's what it is, too much responsibility. You're the only one here Blu responsebility to who for *what*? That's what I mean I say to myself I'm the only one here just me and all these pretty colored bottles, it's me against aaaalll them. *Out numbered!* Well I'll just do my best I guess what the hell awright all you bottles, up against the wall! Oh, you are against the wall...Well, YOU! *Beefeater!* Back! Get back I tell you. No you get outta my hand now... *No!*...Awright well guess you won this round but you just watch yourself, ya hear? I ain't goin no place, *got it!*...Pick up the fountain gun from its rubber holster and shoot a quick blast of bubbles into the drink, squeeze a lime wedge over it cupping my hand in front of the glass for a shield like I've seen Joe do only now there's no one at the bar to shield, and then set the glass on the bar at the place where I was sitting.

There ya go Blu, I say.

Swing back around to my seat.

Well thank ya sir, I reply to myself and take a sip... Ahhhhh...Very nice.

Aim to please we *aim* to please...

On the television in front of me is a program about Great Whites. Rolling blank black button doll eyes and jagged teeth. Pointy streamline snout bumping against the inside glass of the tv. Graceful sexy slithering ballet swimwiggle like a silk scarf shimmering through the deep solid water, stalking...Scarf with jaws that could rip you to shreds...Side to side it swings the long supple back half of its body the way a voluptuous woman's ass shifts and sways its globes like colliding planets, that fleshy bounce and meaty jerk shift of the haunches uncontrollable and uncontrived, just is, just beautiful built-in is. A shark *huge* is being hoisted now by block and tackle from its tailfin onto the deck of a boat. It's dead. A guy is kneeling down and cutting open its long white belly, long incision from throat to anus. With his hand he digs around inside the shark. Looks like he's about to climb inside it the way I've heard half-frozen winter huntsmen will sometimes kill and gut elk and roll inside to stay warm. What's that he's pulling out? Has hold of some crumpled dark thing, tosses it aside. There's another one. Tosses it. I lean forward over my drink to focus in harder on the tv what *are* those?... Seals...Those are seals! Keeps pulling them out like black rabbits out of a sharkskin suit. Creates a small black gnarled mound on the deck. Five now. His arm fishes around in there again. Nothing...looks like that's all of them. Wait no there's another one, six! Six seals he tosses out of that thing, what a gut! And all of them only slightly mangled, undigested. Fresh kill. Was it all one scooping gulp feat of amazing predatory skill or a series of nips that brought that now wasted dinner? Know how it must feel…many a time, at least enough times to where it's distasteful to count, hours after finishing a delightful meal the whole works have been tossed out of me by the manmade arm of alcohol. Useless waste, and now only stomach acid burning the throat and coating the teeth thickly making them feel wooden. Steel blade by any other name does the trick.

Finish the drink and swing around again to make another. Above my head glide two Great Whites through blue in a box. They curl and wiggle and circle, their sawblades just aching to buzz into something. They are waiting, searching, lording through the blue that is their castle world, their planet and realm. They're hungry like they're probably always hungry like I'm always hungry and they want to eat and want to eat *anything*, anything that stumbles into their path they'll tear at and swallow because they have every right because they're hungry and this is their kingdom their domain and anything in their domain has given up its rights to be anything other than prospective food for the lord. Push those teeth through the water like an anxious screen filtering all the smoothness while waiting for that chunky meat thing to clog in them and get stuck for good.

As I glide around the corner of the bar back to my seat Joe comes out, fixes himself a Cutty on the rocks and climbs onto a stool beside me. Circling circling in the blue box continues.

Made awmost a tousand tonight, he says. At's pretty good for a tursday.

He smiles a little and takes a sip from his drink. I can see that he's pleased with himself and he should be, nearly a grand in one night tending bar alone is extraordinary. He's tired though, eyes are droopy. Sure and why not he's not as young as he once was of course. Probably getting around 50 now so of course his energy is waning a little, but so's mine and he's got twenty years on me and I didn't even *do* anything but sit here...

What's this *sharks?* Joe asks.

Yeah they just ripped one open that had six seals inside it.

Six seals huh? Those fuckers are awesome, all just one big muscle an teeth. All they wanna do is eat. They don't care about a goddamn ting those tings but demselves and eating, just not in their nature ta give a shit...Well, I don't know, Joe says, it's not in anyting's nature ta give a shit really when it comes ta livin, is it? We're all just lookin out fer ourselves, ain't we? Don'tcha tink? What else can we do, really...Right?

We're quiet for a while and just watch the television and sip at our drinks. The sharks have decided to go after one of the cameramen who's dropped in the water in a steal cage, ram it repeatedly. Some of the bars are bent and twisted. There are gaps now where the sharks can insert their noses all the way up to the top row of teeth almost. The guy's got balls he still has hold of the camera. Close-up of the spread mouths as they knock the cage and then the shot's thrown all over like a rollercoaster ride. They grab hold of the bars in their teeth and shake their heads and the little steel cell rocks and jerks, throwing the guy around inside. They're trying to toss him out. Hangs on, though. After each attack, and each attack only lasts a few seconds at a time but those are *fierce* seconds, the cameraman adjusts the camera upright again and focuses the shot on the sharks as they circle at a distance. Holds the shot till they attack again.

Me? Joe says. Me I don't care about myself, see…I need someone ta love and take care of, then I'm awright. That's how I look out fer my*self*, see, by needing someone else to love.

Big rolling jaws clenching and ripping, squeezing at those bars with triangle knives, the eyes rolled back into the head…

You know I wasn't always a bartender Blu.

Yeah I know that, I say. You were a school teacher.

Dizzy blue rollercoaster blur vertical bars diagonal bars vertical bars shark tail…

Yeah taught grade school histry, Joe says.

The cage begins to ascend now, the boat on top is hoisting it up. Cameraman clings at the top bars as it rises, looking down. Looks like a frog hanging there. Don't blame those sharks the guy looks like a giant frog dinner. Teasing those things by putting food behind bars when they know their appetite.

Ah fuck this…Come on back here Blu, bring your

drink.

I follow Joe into the backroom and sit at the desk. Still, dense chewy air like inside a bunker. The room is gray with dirty light. The florescent bulb above the desk is half dead. The ends of the tube are dark gray. A hum comes from it. There are no windows and the ceiling is low. Empty beer boxes are stacked and scattered about the floor. On a round tray with a mirror for a bottom that says *Miller* in gold letters Joe cuts line after line with a business card.

Yeah I taught histry, Joe says as he rolls a twenty into a tight tube, six grade...Leans over the tray SSSSNNAHH uh SSN SSN...Lifts his head and pinches his nostrils and sniffs two short sniffs...I had a wife once too, who I'm still in love with, but that was a long time ago. I still see her though, spend most of my days off up at her house in Hercules. Usta be *our* house...SSSSNNAHH...I been tinkin about goin back ta get my teachin certificate again. This...takes a swallow of scotch...this, I'm gett'n too old fer this shit man. Maybe another year the way I see it. I make pretty good money at this place ya know. He stares directly into my eyes and says, I have expensive habits you see. Bends down to the mirror and does another line. The room gets smaller. I set my drink on the desk and water rims along the circle of its bottom. My fingers are wet with condensation from my glass and I run them along my forehead and over my eyelids. The hum from the light is steady. Wonder why he doesn't offer me any? But I tink another year an I'll be out of it he says. I can't keep goin this way man…Does another quick blast…I tink me an my wife could get it goin again once I'm outta here. She always hated my being a bartender. If I get my certificate an start teachin again I tink we'd be awright…

He finishes off the coke and clears the desk, wiping the mirror clean and putting it back inside the desk drawer. I don't know why Joe's said all this to me, and I don't know what to say now that he's said it. All I can see is your face your face your face…

A Mexican woman pokes her head through the door, startles me. Where'd *she* come from!

Hi Ester, come on in, Joe says, and she steps just inside the threshold to a mop stuck in a pail on wheels parked beside the door. She grabs the mop handle and pulls the apparatus toward her, wheels squeaking as she drags it out and across the short hallway into the men's room. That's the only speech Ester leaves us with before getting to work, the squeak of those wheels.

Simultaneously it occurs to us both that with the presence of Ester the night is done. I stand up, leaving my drink unfinished and sweating on the desk. Joe follows me through the bar and lets me out the front door. There's a strange look in his eyes, strange and numb. His jaw's a little slack, bottom teeth showing above the thin lower lip. His eyes seem to say as they look at me: So now you've seen now you know.

Night Blu, he says.

See ya Joe.

I step out. The door closes quickly behind me and I hear the bolt slide into place.

I stand for a moment on the corner looking up into the sky that melts over and into the buildings into the streets unifying heaven and earth in black silence. Slowly I turn and take a few steps up 17th, toward my place. Then in a sudden burst I run, run like mad my hair pinned back against my skull, wind whizzing through my ears and eyelashes. My eyes begin to water from the cool air coming into them and tears stream off my cheekbones. I feel the soles of my work boots slap against the pavement and my heels and thighs begin to ache, but I do not slow down. If anything I go faster. Or imagine I do. My entire body is throbbing. My chest wants to collapse. And I'm laughing. I'm laughing because I want to die but will not allow myself to quit running, because if I stop running the salty fluid pouring out of my eyes will become true tears. I will run, run all the way to my door. I will force life inside of me, inject it into my body through movement, through forcing the night air to rush in my mouth to expand my chest and explode my lungs to shards like bottles.

I run, and night has never been so lonely or beautyful. I run, and it's as if a hard shell is stripping from me like a hood of a car popping up and breaking off, sailing away into the wind like a dead leaf. The wind is purifying fire washing me and I am dissolving in its burn. I run, and the deep murky sadness that touches all of our lives at one point or another, a sadness springing from no place other than that we are here on this earth, that we exist, but exist dubiously, carries with it the ability to silence everything but an unearthly appetite for dream and questions. I run, and there will always be dream and questions.

PRETTY EXPOSED

The bus heads on up the hill. Shit.

Ya just missed it! a woman laughs from inside the glass shelter. Don't see her at first; I'm watching the ass of the bus roll on up the hill. Shit. I come walking up and sit with her in the shelter.

Just missed it! she laughs again.

I know.

You lucky you missed that bus, she says.

Yeah?

Yeah. Now ya get ta meet me, she laughs. Want some? Holds out a tallboy twist-wrapped in a little brown paper bag.

Naw...just had one, I smile, lying.

Awright...Ah'm waitin for ma fren...he late. Ah'm gonna fuck'im too an he late. You believe that? Sheeeeiit, she laughs.

He's late, huh?

Yeaahhh...I need to get fucked too I'm so horny. She takes a slug from the can. I ain't lyin either. You wanna fuck? she laughs and leans over to brush my crotch with the tips of her fingers. I laugh too.

Fuckin makes everything sooo goooood…she says.

I smile at her.

Listen you probly think Ah'm juss playin but Ah'm for *real*. Ah'm so horny Ah'll suck you righ here. Righ here, she says, and slides over a seat next to me. Whaya think? Hmm?

It's pretty bright out, I say. We're pretty exposed here.

Thass awright I know how to do it. Ah'll suck it good too. Ah'll suck it and then Ah'll get up here like this, she jumps off her seat and turns around and leans against the inside glass wall of the shelter with her feet spread apart like she's being frisked, then you could put it here, she says patting her ass, and mmmm we'd go to it.

She laughs and sits back down. There are two hand-prints like ghost stars on the glass.

You know this guy down here on the corner said he'd fuck me…

What guy?

This guy down here on the street when Ah was buyin ma beer…Almos did it too, but he wasn't my type. He wanted to wear a rubber. Sheeeiit…Ah'm clean Ah don't need no rubber gett'n in the way. Hey, Ah'm Calico, she says and puts out her hand.

Blu.

We clasp hands and she holds on. Hey Blu, Ah'm for real baby. Ah need me some. She takes my hand and

cradles it to her breasts and rubs it around. C'mon…
Hey, how bout this. Ah got ten an you got ten an we
fuck an whoever better gets ta keep the othah ten. Ah
know *Ah'm* good. You cain't lose either way.

Who decides?

Who decides what?

Who decides who's better?

We *both* do. C'mon baby…Oh Ah juss wanna suck
it righ here. Bus ain't comin for another twenty minutes. If you take it out Ah swear Ah'll suck it righ here.

What if your man comes?

What man! Ain't *got* no man!

Your friend.

Thass awright he juss ma fren. Ah'll fuck him too,
she laughs.

Those are the best kind of friends, I say.

Thass righ baby.

We laugh together then.

We'll fuck and make looove an fuck an make looove
…Thass righ, the bess kin'a fren…Listen here, see that
doorway crossa street? Ma cousin live righ over there.
We could go over there an fuck. He'd probly let us do it
righ'n his room. Hey, got any change? Yeah, we could
go righ ovah there an fuck. Oooo c'mon daddy
hsssssssss, she hisses and reaches over and messages
my hardon. Oooo daddy *hsssssssss* oh Ah need some
she goes, realizing the firm roll she has in her hand. She
gets up and stands between my knees. I let her go right
on rubbing it.

She leans in to put my crotch against hers and bends her mouth to my ear. I catch the smell of beer and body odor.

C'mon daddy, she moans, fuck meeeeeee. Her tongue mops inside my ear. A shudder runs through me always loved that. I reach out and tickle her crotch.

You really need it bad, huh?

Oh daddy *hsssssssss*...You got any change? Ah wanna get some weed.

Sure you don't wanna buy a rock?

Ahownt smoke rock.

Why don'tcha just go over there and fuck your cousin?

Ahownt do that. Come on, less get some weed'n go over there'n do it. Gotta five? Ah could get some weed righ down the street.

What's this? I ask flicking her protruding nipple. Baby you ain't got nothin on under there, I say.

She lifts up her teal blue sweatshirt as she stands before me and shows her brown breast then quickly covers it again. Some people pass behind the shelter and she makes an uh-oh face at them. When they're gone she undoes the button of her jeans, opens the fly, waves her hips. I run a finger down her smooth chocolate bunny belly and up and down through her pubic hair. Feels like soft brushed-out felt. I'd give the sugar of her belly a lick if it wasn't for the odor.

Her dark fingers disappear inside her open fly and retrieve a thin glaze which she smears on the back of my hand. It's warm then turns cool in the breeze on my skin. She fumbles at my zipper.

Here, watch this, Ah'm gonna do it good…oooo… she says, rubbing my erection the whole time. Doan worry bout it, no one'll see. Ah know how to do it…

Whatcha gonna do?

Ah'm gonna suck it.

No no, not here, and I zip back up.

C'mooon dad*dyyy* lemme do it…

I sit there facing the street. Over her shoulder I see faces staring out through car windows looking at us moshing groins in the bus shelter as they roll by up and down the hill. It's Sunday early afternoon. I'm in the Western Edition at the edge of the Fillmore. Some of those faces may be coming straight from Sunday worship. Baptist churches abound in this area. A smile curls beneath my dark sunglasses. Even she hasn't seen my eyes. Her lips are like two copulating dew worms glistening. She leans in to my ear again.

Give me a five daddy…Ah'm good for it.

I reach into my pocket and give her some change.

C'mon, less get some weed'n go do it…

I don't respond.

Whassamatter? Ah'm single, you're single…Right? You're single?

The question strikes my heart.

Yeah, I say. I'm single.

Wull come on then.

She starts rubbing it real good now. There's the very

real threat of exploding in my pants. I laugh.

C'mon daddy, gimme five.

I laugh some more.

Ah'm gonna come righ here then.

She straddles my thigh.

Ah ain't playin Ah'm gonna come.

I laugh, laugh. Go ahead baby, come.

Ah'm gonna…And she sets down to it, wriggling on my thigh.

But just then as she starts to really move and dig in she goes, Sheeeiit…here come da bus, and stands up off me and buttons her pants but leaves the fly alone. Give me a five baby…Gimme two… *One* then…

I laugh and give her the rest of my change. The bus comes to a stop and the door swings open. I pat her well-rounded bottom. Hope you get some baby, I say, and laughing step up onto the bus.

Oh Ah weell, ya *damn* shore know that…

And I roll away up the hill laughing laughing as I ascend, light, lighter, leave her to her Shiva dance.